From the Pages of

THREE THEBAN PLAYS

Do you even know your provenance?
You are unaware that you are the enemy of your kin
both beneath and above the earth, unaware
that the double-edged curse of your mother and father
will one day fiercely drive you from this land in darkness,
though now your eyes can see.

(from *Oedipus the King*, ll. 404–409)

But whoever is haughty in word or deed,
ignoring justice, not revering
the shrines of the gods:
may evil fortune seize him for his ill-fated pride.

(from *Oedipus the King*, ll. 844–847)

Unfortunate man, may you never find out who you are.

(from *Oedipus the King*, l. 1022)

He tore off the golden pins
that fastened her dress, raised them high, and plunged them
into the sockets of his eyes, crying out that now his eyes
would see neither his suffering nor his evil deeds.

(from *Oedipus the King*, ll. 1231–1234)

Dwellers of our native city of Thebes, behold! This is Oedipus,
who solved the infamous riddle and was the most mighty of men,
on whose fortune no citizen could look without envy,
but who was overtaken by a wave of dreadful disaster!

(from *Oedipus the King*, ll. 1445–1448)

Alas, miserable wretch that I am! Where can I flee?
What gods can help me, what mortals?

(from *Oedipus at Colonus*, ll. 789–790)

Not to be born is the condition
that surpasses all others.
But once man is born,
the next best thing is to return
with utmost haste to where he has come from.
For even youth with all its airy thoughtlessness
finds that ample suffering
is never far away.

(from *Oedipus at Colonus*, ll. 1197–1204)

I shall lie, beloved, with my beloved brother, having committed
a pious crime, since the time I must please those below
is far longer than the time I must please those here above.

(from *Antigone*, ll. 65–67)

No baser custom ever arose among men
than money. It sacks cities and uproots men from their houses.
It is a masterful teacher in perverting the minds of just men,
inciting them to turn to disgraceful deeds.

(from *Antigone*, ll. 286–289)

Why should I, wretched as I am, still look to the gods?
Which of the gods can I appeal to, when it was
through my pious act that I have been charged with impiety?

(from *Antigone*, ll. 885–887)

Alas! My disastrous judgment!
Woe, my son, young in your untimely death,
Ai ai! Ai ai!
You are dead, you are gone,
not because of your bad judgment
but because of mine.

(from *Antigone*, ll. 1206–1211)

THREE THEBAN PLAYS

OEDIPUS THE KING

✦

OEDIPUS AT COLONUS

✦

ANTIGONE

SOPHOCLES

TRANSLATED BY

PETER CONSTANTINE

With an Introduction and Notes
by Pedro de Blas

GEORGE STADE

CONSULTING EDITORIAL DIRECTOR

BARNES & NOBLE CLASSICS

NEW YORK

Barnes & Noble Classics
New York

Published by Barnes & Noble Books
122 Fifth Avenue
New York, NY 10011

www.barnesandnoble.com/classics

Antigone was first produced in 442 or 441 B.C., *Oedipus the King* sometime between 430 and 428 B.C., and *Oedipus at Colonus* in 402 or 401 B.C.

Published in 2007 by Barnes & Noble Classics in a new translation with new Introduction, Note on the Translator, Notes, Biography, Chronology, Inspired By, Comments & Questions, and For Further Reading.

Three Theban Plays
ISBN-13: 978-1-59308-235-2
ISBN-10: 1-59308-235-5
LC Control Number 2007927682

Produced and published in conjunction with:
Fine Creative Media, Inc.
322 Eighth Avenue
New York, NY 10001

Michael J. Fine, President and Publisher

Printed in the United States of America

QM

9 11 13 15 14 12 10 8

SOPHOCLES

Sophocles—along with Aeschylus and Euripides one of the three greatest of the ancient Greek writers of dramatic tragedy whose works have come down to us—was born around 497 B.C. in the village of Colonus Hippius, just outside Athens. His father, Sophilos, is believed to have been a wealthy arms dealer. Sophocles was educated in the arts and won awards for both music and wrestling. His industriousness, or perhaps the humming smoothness of the language in his plays, earned him the nickname "Attic Bee," and his physical beauty and grace of character were also notable; in his play *The Frogs*, Aristophanes described Sophocles as "good natured." In 480 he led the boys' chorus in the victory celebration in Athens of the defeat of the Persians in the battle of Salamis.

By 468 Sophocles had completed his studies and was prepared to enter the City Dionysia, a theatrical festival held every March in Athens; his play *Triptolemus* won first place, defeating an entry by Aeschylus. He would write about 120 more plays, winning first prize for about eighteen and never coming in less than second for the rest. In this period—Greece's Golden Age—Sophocles was influenced by the currents of skepticism, empiricism, and relativism that were running through formal thinking and politics; the lives of his characters are governed more by their own flaws than by the gods.

Sophocles brought many innovations to Greek theater. He dispensed with telling a tragic tale in three separate plays, packing an entire story into one drama. Around 460 he introduced a third actor (previously only two appeared on the stage at one time). He used longer stretches of dialogue and reduced the importance of the chorus, although he increased the number of chorus members to fifteen from twelve. He was also the first to use painted background scenes, and he introduced the heroic maiden (such as Antigone and Electra) and the ingenuous young man (Haemon).

For many years Sophocles held the priesthood of the healing gods Alcon and Asclepius. He is credited with introducing the cult of Asclepius to Athens in response to the suffering brought on by the great plague during the early years of the Peloponnesian War (431–404); he turned over his house for Asclepius' worship while a proper temple was being built.

In 443 and 442 Sophocles held the post of *hellenotamias*, one of the state treasurers who controlled the funds of the Delian League. In 441 he produced *Antigone*, whose success may have helped his election as a general, along with the great Greek statesman Pericles, in the Samian War (440–439). He produced *Trachiniae* in the mid 430s and served as general again during the first ten years of the Peloponnesian War. He produced *Oedipus the King* around 429, and *Electra* around 420. In 413 he became a member of a committee of ten older citizens (*probouloi*) that later played a part in establishing a temporary oligarchy in Athens. In 409 he produced *Philoctetes*, winning first prize in the City Dionysia.

Sophocles died in 405. *Oedipus at Colonus* was produced around 401 by his grandson.

TABLE OF CONTENTS

The World of Sophocles and
THREE THEBAN PLAYS

c.497 Sophocles is born in Colonus Hippius, a small town just outside Athens, on a peninsula jutting into the Aegean Sea that today is in central Greece. His father, Sophilos, is a trader in arms, and the family is wealthy. Sophocles is sent to school in Athens and educated in poetry, dance, music, and wrestling; he wins awards in the latter two. During this period Greek city-states are governed by democracies rather than family groups or dictators. Athens is emerging as the premier power among these entities, though wars with Persia and Sparta, a rival city-state, often erupt. The Sophists, traveling teacher/philosophers, promote rationalist thinking that begins to undermine the dominance of myth and religion over the way people think.

c.495 Pericles, the great Greek general and Athenian leader, is born; he will oversee Athenian democracy as it reaches its zenith and become a personal friend of Sophocles.

494 Persian armies sack Miletus, an old Ionian city deeply connected to Athens, enslaving most of the people and deporting them to the Persian Gulf.

c.493 The Athenian tragic poet Phrynichus produces *Capture of Miletus* and is fined 1,000 drachmae for recalling such a painful episode in the misfortunes of Athens' kindred people.

490 The Greeks defeat the Persians for the first time on land in the battle of Marathon. The tragic playwright Aeschylus fights with the Athenians, who outfox the Persians, despite being outnumbered two to one; the victory sparks enormous pride and confidence in Athenians. The pre-Socratic philosopher Empedocles is born around this time.

486 Comic drama is introduced at City Dionysia, Athens' annual religious theater festival held in late March, in which people from all over the region come to drink and celebrate spring. All classes of citizens are welcome, and there is a fund for those who cannot pay. The festival recognizes distinguished citizens, displays the tribute paid to Athens by its subject allies, and on the final day awards prizes to the plays that have been presented. The winning poet receives a crown of ivy.

484 Aeschylus has his first victory in a dramatic contest. Herodotus is born; known as the "father of history" for his *Histories*, he will examine Persian aggression against the Greek city-states through narratives of the period and thorough investigations of the places and people he encounters in his travels around the Mediterranean and Africa. The tragic playwright Euripides is born around this time.

480 The Greeks defeat the Persians on land in the battle of Salamis, in which Aeschylus again fights. Sophocles is chosen to lead the boys' chorus at the Athenian celebration of this victory. The Greek philosopher of nature Anaxagoras moves to Athens; a close friend of Pericles, he will discover the true cause of eclipses, which previously were viewed as powerful bad omens.

479 The Persians continue to try to conquer sites on mainland Greece, but they are defeated at the battle of Plataea by the Spartan general Pausanias, with help from the Athenians.

478 A confederation of Greek city-states forms the Delian League, which collects tribute from its members in exchange for protection from Persian aggression. The league eventually will come under the total control of the Athenians.

476 Phrynichus produces *Phoenician Women*.

c.475 The mathematician Pythagoras of Samos dies; his work is fundamental to geometry.

472 Funded and produced by Pericles, Aeschylus' *Persians* wins first prize at the City Dionysia festival.

470 The great Athenian philosopher Socrates is born.

468 Sophocles submits his first play, *Triptolemus*, to the City Dionysia, taking first prize.

467 Aeschylus' *Seven against Thebes* wins first prize at the City Dionysia.

c.463 Aeschylus' *Suppliant Women* wins first prize.

462 Ephialtes, Athens' leading pro-democracy crusader, curbs the power of the Areopagus, a conservative body of leaders, by introducing reforms to the democratic constitution, which expands the franchise of Athenian citizens and provides more opportunities for political involvement to greater numbers of men, regardless of economic class.

461 Ephialtes is assassinated. His deputy, Pericles, takes over political leadership in Athens, launching Greece's Periclean Age, in which Athens' cultural, military, and political ingeniousness flower.

460 Sophocles introduces a third actor to his plays around this time (previously only two appeared on the stage at one time). Thucydides is born; in writing *History of the Peloponnesian War*, for which he will consult written documents and interview participants in the events, he will become the first truly objective historian. Hippocrates of Kos is born; known as the "father of medicine," he will establish medicine as a branch of science, rejecting the superstition and magic that previously underlay it. Democritus, a geometer and proponent of atomic theory, is born.

458 Aeschylus' *Oresteia* wins first prize at the City Dionysia festival.

456 Aeschylus dies at Gela in Sicily.

455 Euripides first enters the City Dionysia, with *Peliades*.

451 In an attempt to curb the power of aristocrats and contain power in Athens, Pericles introduces a citizenship law that allows only the child of two Athenian citizens to become a full citizen.

c.450 Aristophanes is born.

449 The City Dionysia festival establishes a prize for the best tragic actor.

443 For the next two years Sophocles will serve as *hellenotamias* (imperial treasurer) of the Delian League. Pericles is elected general, as he will be every year until he dies.

441 Sophocles produces *Antigone*. Along with Pericles, he is elected general and charged with putting down the revolt of Samos, one of three independent allies of Athens, which refuses to break off its attacks against Miletus. In his first victory, Euripides takes first place over Sophocles in the City Dionysia.

438 Euripides' *Alcestis* wins second prize in the City Dionysia.

430s Sophocles produces *Trachiniae*. The Parthenon, the temple of Athena Parthenos, is dedicated on the Acropolis at Athens. Designed by Greek architects Iktinos and Kallikrates, it has taken more than fifteen years to build and is the principal element in Pericles' building program, which is being overseen by the sculptor Phidias. At about this time Phidias also produces what will be named one of the seven wonders of the ancient world, the Statue of Zeus at Olympia—a seated statue of Zeus made of ivory and gold.

431 The Peloponnesian War breaks out between the two regional empires Athens and Sparta, when Sparta invades Attica, the countryside around Athens. Sophocles serves as general during the first phase of the conflict, known as the Archidamian War, which lasts more than ten years. Euripides' *Medea* wins third prize in the City Dionysia festival.

430 Plague breaks out in Athens. Phidias, the greatest sculptor in ancient Greece and Pericles' close friend, dies. The philosopher Empedocles, proponent of the theory that all matter is made of earth, air, fire, and water, dies.

c.429 Sophocles produces *Oedipus the King*. Euripides produces *Children of Heracles*.

429 Pericles dies of the plague. The greatest leader of ancient

Greece, he planted the roots of democracy more deeply than any other; much of the glorious art and architecture in Athens resulted from Pericles' vision and ability to fund such projects.

428 Euripides' *Hippolytus* wins first prize at the City Dionysia. Plato is born at about this time. As a follower of Socrates, he will come to be considered one of the most important philosophers who ever lived. Among other things, he will record in dialogue form the teachings of Socrates after he dies, conveying the Socratic method of inquiry, form an academy to educate future rulers, write a parable of Atlantis, and propose the idea of the philosopher king.

425 Aristophanes produces *Acharnians*. Euripides produces *Andromache* at about this time. Herodotus dies.

424 Aristophanes produces *Knights*. Thucydides is appointed a general and given command of a squadron of seven ships.

423 Aristophanes produces *Clouds*.

422 Aristophanes produces *Wasps*.

421 Sparta and Athens sign the Peace of Nicias, marking the end of the first phase of the Peloponnesian War. Aristophanes produces *Peace*, which includes a satire of the agreement.

c.420 Sophocles produces *Electra*.

415 Athens launches an expedition to help Sicily in its war against Selinus. In what will be a two-year, colossal disaster, Athens loses much of its fleet, 25,000 sailors, 9,000 hoplites (soldiers), and many of its subject city-states, who ally with Sparta. Euripides' *Trojan Women* wins second prize at the City Dionysia.

414 Aristophanes produces *Birds*.

c.414 Euripides produces *Iphegenia among the Taurians* at about this time.

412 Euripides produces *Helen*.

411 In the Revolution of the Four Hundred, Athenian democracy is overthrown by a group known as the Oligarchs. Sophocles is thought to have been involved with this coup, due to his membership in the *probouloi*, a committee of ten citizens that preceded the upheaval. Aristophanes produces *Lysistrata* and *Women Celebrating the Thesmophoria*.

409 Sophocles produces *Philoctetes* and wins first prize in the City Dionysia.

408 Euripides produces *Orestes*.

406 The battle of Arginusae, in which Athens pits its slave-manned, newly constructed ships against Sparta, results in an unexpected victory for Athens. In gratitude, the citizens vote to allow the slaves who had fought in the battle to become citizens. Euripides dies.

406–405 Sophocles writes *Oedipus at Colonus*.

405 Sophocles dies.

404 Athens surrenders to Sparta, ending the Peloponnesian War.

c.401 *Oedipus at Colonus* is produced by Sophocles' grandson (also named Sophocles).

INTRODUCTION

Most of us think of theater today as cultural entertainment bought at the price of an admission ticket. But even if theater is regarded purely as entertainment, it still seems to be a special sort of activity: It requires a deliberate effort and expense; it demands a high level of concentration on the part of actors and audience alike (for every performance is, strictly speaking, unique); it develops a particular bond between audience and actors, directors and playwrights; and it can strengthen or challenge social values and attitudes. Other performance-related cultural products, such as movies or television, may achieve similar effects, but those of theater seem to reach further, perhaps because of the immediacy and uniqueness of live performances, regardless of the intrinsic merit of the play. Even plays that we did not enjoy "stay with us" for a while, probably because most of us remember actions carried out by other humans in our physical proximity better than the flickering of light on a screen, regardless of its brightness and its size. Good plays even make us think about them afterward for a long time. An extraordinary play may even contain lines that are quoted later in different contexts, or characters, like Othello or Pygmalion, who acquire an independent life in our imagination.

But what makes a play a good play? Like any art form, theater needs to be understood in its own terms, and those of theater (drama, scene, tragedy) readily refer us to the origins of theater in ancient Greece, and to Athenian tragedy in particular, both as an art form and as a civic activity that the Greeks themselves already valued as the highest manner of public performance.

There are both many similarities and many differences between ancient Greek and modern theater in general, but there is also a remarkable connection between the cultural phenomenon of the theater as it appears today and drama as it was written and produced in Greece nearly twenty-five centuries ago—a connection, by the way, that is not only discussed by scholars, but also deeply felt and exploited by contemporary playwrights (and screenwriters) from different parts of the world. Sometimes the connection seems prodigiously to bridge centuries and continents: In 2003, the Brooklyn Academy of Music included in its program a performance of *The Island*, a play written by Athol Fugard and by the two actors John Kani and Winston Ntshona. *The Island*, a play severely critical of the repressive regime of apartheid in South Africa, was originally rehearsed and performed in secret in Cape Town but made it to the Royal Theatre in London in 1974, and was again acclaimed in New York almost thirty years later. The New York production (which used minimal stage props, but featured Kani and Ntshona in unforgettable performances) delivered a powerful message about the unending need to fight for and to preserve human freedom under repressive governments that rule by fear. The plot of *The Island* develops around the efforts of two prisoners to take advantage of a special occasion in prison life in order to stage Sophocles' *Antigone*. The reasons for that choice will become obvious to the readers of this volume.

Understanding Greek tragedy is not a simple task. Scholarly research on Greek tragedy is very active, and there are still many areas of disagreement among the experts. In this introduction, I make no claims to comprehensive treatment or to revolutionary interpretation; rather, I have done my best to present a condensed summary of current views about the production and interpretation of classical Athenian tragedy. I also point out for first-time readers a few key differences from modern dramatic writing and some interpretive leads about each of the three plays included here. When a point seemed somewhat contentious or out of the general domain of knowledge about tragedy, I have inserted the relevant source in a footnote. In addition, any reader who wishes to learn more about tragedy may refer to the For Further Reading section at the end of this volume. My hope remains that he or she will read the plays carefully first.

GODS, CITIZENS, AND CHORUSES

Greek Plays and Their Performance

From a historical perspective, Greek tragedy means the theatrical works produced mainly in Greece during the fifth century B.C.E.[1] Tragedies were produced during religious festivals in honor of the god Dionysos, the most important of which was the one known as the City Dionysia, held in Athens every year. Comedy also played an important role in those festivals, but comic plays were given much less time in the total program, and the Greeks themselves considered them, rightly or wrongly, a lesser form of poetical creation. During their heyday in the fifth century, the festivals would last seven days, from dawn till dusk, and would be celebrated with exceptional enthusiasm. They marked a time for looser behavior, for drinking and the blurring of social distinctions, much like the later Roman saturnalia or our modern-day Mardi Gras. Ambassadors and other public figures would take advantage of the opportunity to make public announcements, and there was a general atmosphere of social inclusion and celebration of the greatness of Athens.

On the first day of the festival, the statue of Dionysus would be taken from the temple to the theater, where it would remain until the last day. The tragic trilogies, however, would not begin until the third day, since the second day was devoted to a contest of songs in the form of dithyrambs (songs of the "two doors") sung by a chorus in honor of Dionysos, a Greek god who was born twice, once from Semele, a Theban woman loved by Zeus, whose fire burned her to ashes, and again from Zeus himself, after he had sewn Dionysos inside his own leg in order to carry him to term. The "double birth" of Dionysos is only one of the many mysterious features of this god who, after springing from Zeus' thigh, becomes a wandering deity, a god of nowhere who seeks to be respected wherever he travels. It seems that the early singers of dithyrambs celebrated him through disguising themselves as animals by wearing goatskins. The goatskins may explain the name *tragoidia* ("song of the goat") for these performances, a name that was later extended to the tragic plays themselves, after the format of the play began to develop when the Athenian Thespis introduced an actor who interrupts the choral song and starts to have a dialogue with the dithyrambic chorus. Or perhaps the tragoidia has to do with the sacrifice of a goat on the occasion, and not with the goatskins at all. In any event, the main trend today is not to focus on the precise terms of the connection with Dionysos, but on understanding tragedy as an art form, and on its social, moral, and political aspects.

Starting on the third day of the City Dionysia festival, a tetralogy formed by a tragic trilogy plus a satyr play would be performed every day of the next three. The satyr play was probably intended as comic relief or as a lighter way to reinforce or comment on the message of the tragedies that it accompanied. At the end of the festival, one tetralogy would be chosen as the winner, as would one of the five comedies that were produced on the sixth day. The tragedies of Aeschylus, Sophocles, and Euripides, and the comedies of Aristophanes were all produced at such festivals, although not all of the surviving plays won first prize. (Students of tragedy should remember that we have only a very small number of the plays that were produced.)

Large public events, then as now, cost large sums of money, and the City Dionysia was probably the largest annual gathering in Athens. Since the festival was held in March, at the beginning of the sailing season in the Aegean Sea, it is safe to say that these events may have been the largest gatherings in the ancient Greek world, with city dwellers, farmers from the region of Attica, and foreign visitors all in attendance. The admission price was affordable to an average person, and there was also a public fund known as the *theoria* (from *theorein*, meaning "to see") that financed the admission price for those who could not afford it. The Athenians seem to have been truly concerned with making dramatic performances accessible to everyone.

In order to finance the tragic festivals, the Athenians operated a system known as "liturgies." Under this system, a wealthy citizen would be designated by the top magistrate (the *archon*) to pay all expenses attendant to the production of one of the three trilogies chosen by the archon several months before the tragedy contest. Although the financing of plays seems to have conferred a degree of social status in ancient Athens, if the person designated (known as the *choregos*) believed that someone else was in a better financial position to bear the cost, he could suggest his name. The person so named could then either bear the expenses in question or offer to swap his assets with the citizen who had named him.

Once the identity of the choregos had been confirmed, he had to recruit and pay the chorus (on which more later), and buy the masks, special "platform" footwear (*cothurni*), and costumes that would be worn by the actors, and make arrangements for the rehearsals. He also had to hire singers and musicians, for Greek tragedies were written in verse, and as was the case with most ancient poetry, substantial parts were sung with musical accompaniment. Unfortunately, that music has been lost to us, but we should remember that the audience of a Greek tragedy did not sit in a dark theater listening to words alone, but celebrated a god, in daylight and open air, while the chorus and sometimes the actors sang many of their lines.

The actors (all male, even those who played female characters) were originally chosen by the author himself, but from the middle of the fifth century the *archon* chose the main actor, who would form a company for the play in question. Both the actors and the author were paid with public funds, not by the choregos. On the first day of the festival, the author and actors would present the plays, in an act known as *proagon*. We don't know exactly what went on during those presentations, which were perhaps a sort of ancient version of our movie trailers, but we do know that they afforded an opportunity to see the actors without masks, and perhaps to learn which actor would play which character—or rather characters, because the number of actors on stage was initially limited to two and later (with Sophocles) to three, but there was no limit on the number of characters. The number of speaking parts in a tragedy was often close to eight, and the necessary entrances and exits in the play indicate that actors often played more than one character. The versatility of the ancient actors is to be admired, even though the use of masks must have helped somewhat.

In addition to the peculiarities of ancient Greek dramatic productions noted above, something more fundamental is also different between Greek tragedy and our modern theatrical productions, namely the expectations about the novelty of the plot. Today we expect new plays to surprise us with stories of characters or at least places or situations previously unheard of. Such novelty would have never occurred to an ancient playwright: Greek audiences were used to knowing the plot of the story in advance, something that was possible thanks to the widespread knowledge of myth.

Myth, in this sense, includes not only the stories about the birth and deeds of the different Greek gods, but also the stories told in the Homeric epic poems *Iliad* and *Odyssey* about the Trojan War and its aftermath (the Trojan epic cycle forms the basis of the plot of more than half of the extant tragedies) and the adventures of characters like Hercules or Jason, as well as the stories of the tragic families of the Atreidae of Argos and the Labdacidae of Thebes (including Oedipus and his descendants). The Greeks knew much more than we do about those stories. We can only learn about them from sources such as Homer, Hesiod, the tragedians themselves, and later mythographers, both Greek and Roman. The Greeks, however, had access to a significant oral tradition of poetry that enabled them to appreciate the twists of the tragic plots better than we will ever be able to. Many readers will know the name of Zeus, the supreme Greek god, but other deities may not be so familiar today. In this edition, they have been identified, along with place names and other terms, in the notes when they first appear in each play.

In fifth-century Athens, there was no gospel-like account available of the mythical stories, but rather many different versions of them, as well as further refinements and interpretive retellings by the tragedians, who sometimes changed details of the mainstream versions or filled continuity gaps. For example, the plot of Euripides' *Helen* draws on a mythical tradition (attested by the historian Herodotus in the second book of his *Histories*) according to which the real Helen was not abducted to Troy, but sat out the Trojan war in Egypt, while a ghost took her place in Troy. Therefore, in stark contrast with the Homeric version of the story, in Euripides' play the two Helens appear together, and Menelaos has to decide who is the real one. In addition to being an ancient forerunner of the literary device of the doppelganger, the play obviously assumes a familiarity with different versions of the story of Helen's abduction. We don't know how many there were. More generally, we can never assume that we know as much as a Greek audience did about the background of the tragic plots, or of any other kind of Greek poetry.

If we bear in mind all the above, it is relatively easy to understand why the dramatic competitions engaged the collective memory of the city, and why their staging and attendance were both a religious and a civic duty. All male citizens would be in the audience, of course, thereby making tragedy into a more open and democratic art form than the more restricted recitals of epic or lyric poetry, which were intended for smaller audiences. Attendance by women remains an open question. Some scholars believe that they were excluded from the dramatic festivals, but some comedies contain direct addresses to the women in the audience, which would seem to point to some level of female attendance at least at comic plays.

Seating within the area of the theater (*theatron*) allocated to each *deme* (an administrative division originally based on geographical divisions) was not assigned, with the exception of the front row, which was reserved for the priests of Zeus and Apollo, magistrates, and ambassadors. Foreigners who had performed a special service for Athens were also sometimes given the right (known as *proedria*) to sit in the front row, as were the sons of Athenian citizens who had died in combat on behalf of the city. The priest of Dionysos sat in the center of the front row. All seats, however, afforded a good view, and the acoustics of Greek theaters ensured that the play could be enjoyed even from the highest seats of the amphitheater, which was semicircular in shape, with the seats placed on the side of a hill. This shape and design is still in use today—for instance, at the Olivier Theatre within the Royal National Theatre in London.

FROM THE THEATER TO THE PAGE
Hints on Reading a Greek Tragedy

The action of a Greek tragedy took place in a circular area about 65 feet in diameter, called the *orchestra* (a word etymologically associated with dancing) that was accessed by the actors and the chorus through ramps *(parodoi)* on either side. The one on the right represented the way toward the city, while the one on the left was used when exiting away from it (for example, toward the sea). Slightly elevated above the orchestra was the *logeion*, on which the actors stood and spoke.

The chorus was a group of dancers (twelve before Sophocles, fifteen afterward, divided in two groups of seven, plus a chorus leader) with a multifarious participation in the play. A chorus was made up of male citizens, and it was considered an honor for young men to serve in one, although membership in the chorus, like acting, later became professionalized. In the early tragedies, the chorus engages in dialogue with the characters, and becomes one more character, so to speak, who perhaps represents the point of view of the citizens of the relevant city, the author, or the most predictable reactions of the audience. Later on, the chorus still comments on the action, but tends not to engage in dialogue with the actors.

When reading a Greek tragedy, it is important to remember that the entrance of the chorus, the choral songs (known as *stasima*, commonly three or four in every play), and the exit song are written in lyric meters that suit the emotional content of the lines; these sections often express undiluted anguish or horror. In contrast, the lines of dialogue are most often written in iambic trimeter, the meter that was closest to the spoken Athenian dialect, according to Aristotle. (As a parallel for readers who do not know Greek, it may help to recall that Shakespeare's iambic pentameter is the closest meter to natural speech in English.)

The characters, we should also note, are not characters in a modern sense, and this too creates a difficulty in reading Greek tragedy: The characters lack a full psychology and are rather a collection of reactions to the events of the play. Obviously, this is consistent with the use of masks and clothes that probably gave no clue about a local or temporal setting, because no clue was needed. Many modern readers find this alienating, because today we are used to stories that introduce the characters to us and give us all sorts of details about them. We should remember that the Greek audience already knew the characters and the details of the story—one reason why it is helpful to be familiar with the plot of the tragedies before reading them. Plot summaries for the tragedies in this volume are included below.

Several items were used for the ancient Greek version of special effects. The first is the *ekkyklema*, probably a sort of stretcher on wheels that would be used, for example, to roll the "corpse" of a character onto the stage at the appropriate moment. The second is the *mechane*, a crane that would be used to suspend an actor above the *skene*, a hut that was placed on the stage and was used by the actors to change costumes and masks, and that possibly also served to represent a building as required by the action of the play. Gods and goddesses could appear in the play suspended in mid-air by the mechane (whence the expression *deus ex machina*) in order to settle disputes or otherwise bring the action of the play to a close.

Today we enjoy Greek tragedy mainly as literature, although theater listings in major cities often contain productions of Greek tragedy in translation or adaptations of the ancient plays. The music, the singing, and the special effects are lost to us, but we should remember that they were worked out in detail by the Greeks, and that the show was probably much less static than some modern productions would lead us to believe. As readers, we should keep in mind that there were at the most only three actors simultaneously on stage. It is best to keep track exactly of who is on stage at any time. For this reason, this edition marks the entrances and exits, even though neither these nor any other stage directions are given in the Greek texts.

TRAGIC ERRORS AND THEIR REALIZATION
The Theory of Tragedy

We have only a few of the hundreds of tragedies that were written and produced in classical Greece, and only one complete trilogy. We have complete works by only three playwrights (Aeschylus, Sophocles, and Euripides) out of the many more who competed in the ancient festivals. In addition, tragedies were written in highly stylized and therefore difficult Greek, with the result that scholars often disagree about the correct interpretation of one tragedy or another as a whole or of particular scenes within them. There are even occasional disagreements about which of two characters speaks a few lines of dialogue, a matter on which the medieval manuscripts with copies of the plays (our main textual source) are silent.

Thus it is difficult to say anything conclusive about ancient Greek tragedy in general as an art form. Nevertheless, it seems beyond doubt that the plays were very powerful dramatic creations. They still engage us deeply by means of the complex interplay between the characters and the weighty and multifaceted moral questions they pose. Even modern audiences who are not familiar with the plots in advance are unavoidably moved when they are confronted with, for example, Medea killing her own children out of vengeful wrath against Jason, or with Oedipus blinding himself after discovering the truth about the murder of his father and about his wife's identity.

Greek thinkers were the first to take tragedy into consideration as an art form with great social and political relevance. As a prominent Athenian citizen, Plato must have been in the audience of some of the extant plays, and it is very likely that he knew famous tragedians personally; nevertheless, his views on tragedy do not seem to have been altogether positive. In Plato's *Republic*, the ideal city that Socrates imagines during his conversation with Glaucon has no place for poetry in general, nor for tragedy in particular. Socrates sees a danger in tragedy, because it makes the audience react to the events of the play as if they were real, and derive moral lessons from them. This is undesirable, in Socrates' view, because such events are at two removes from reality: first, because they are poetic creations of events, and not the events themselves; second, because even the actual events of life are not real in the sense of presenting us with the truth. The truth, according to Socrates, exists only in another dimension, in the realm of the Forms, which only the philosophers know, because their souls have gained access to them in the afterlife before their reincarnation and return to terrestrial life.

Obviously, behind this very contrived and infamous condemnation of poetry, there is an elitist fear of public opinion. The Socratic position is based on a particular sort of belief in the afterlife and reincarnation of the soul, together with a strong apprehension about the potential of tragedy to inspire civic dialogue about the collective past, traditional values, and current politics. We have already seen how tragedy was part and parcel of the Athenian democratic way of life. For Socrates, the tragic festivals, together with the public trials, were paramount examples of collective foolishness made into a public virtue.

That is not all there is to Plato's views on tragedy. In the *Laws*, his last dialogue, Plato moderates his views somewhat. He is still very afraid of the democratic traits and consensus-building potential of tragedy, but the pragmatism he exhibits in this last major work makes it impossible to ban theater from the city. The (nameless) Athenian, the main speaker in this dialogue, from which Socrates is completely absent, adopts a different position: First, he defends the legal code he has constructed in the dialogue as the perfect way of ordering a society, and gives reasons for every law he proposes; second, he sees tragedy as an alternative way to generate moral conviction among the citizens—but without giving proper argumentative reasons for such conviction. Therefore, tragedy will be allowed, provided that it does not contradict any of the provisions of the legal code, which is a perfect creation, according to the Athenian. That is how the exclusion of tragedy by Socrates in the *Republic* is replaced by a strict system of censorship in the *Laws*. Neither of the two approaches worked in practice; tragedy remained successful in the classical period, and the quality of the plays that are extant suggests that the Athenian public did, in fact, develop a consistent and demanding theatrical taste that seemed to favor the playwrights' willingness to present them with challenging questions.

Aristotle was not an Athenian, and the productions of most of the extant tragedies pre-dated his presence in the city. Therefore, he probably knew less than Plato about tragedy and tragedians firsthand; nevertheless, he also wrote about tragedy at length in his *Poetics*, but his approach is very different from Plato's. He is not concerned with the potentially negative effects of tragedy, but accepts it as a fact of life in Greek society. His project is simply to analyze tragedy as an artistic phenomenon, in order to understand the internal reasons for its success. With the *Poetics*, Aristotle inaugurates Western literary criticism, for which that work remains mandatory reading.

For Aristotle too, tragedy is an imitation of reality, but an imitation that is closer to reality than epic or lyric poetry, since tragic characters act on their own initiative, and are not guided by and under the constant tutelage of the gods. In a tragedy, the main character somehow confronts the uncertainty of the future alone, and is faced with all sorts of questions, including some that are of current relevance (for example, the conduct of a war or the development of a legal system as a mechanism of social regulation) and others that are larger than himself or herself (such as the ultimate aim of human action or the irresistible desire to know the truth about the past).

An essential element of tragedy, for Aristotle, is the "reversal of fortune" (*peripeteia*). The tragic hero must change between states of fortune and misfortune. This reversal comes about because of the "error" (*hamartia*) of the tragic hero. Traditionally, the word hamartia was understood as a tragic flaw that was inherent to the character, but today the consensus seems to be shifting toward a restrictive interpretation of the term, in line with what Aristotle says in the *Ethics* about mistakes due to ignorance (*hamartema*, a word with a very close meaning in Greek to hamartia).[2] What matters are not the hero's personal traits or whether his/her actions are morally right or wrong, but the fact that he/she does something in error, whether in respect to the action itself, the persons affected, the means of the action, or the result intended. Aristotle also makes clear that it is necessary that the tragic hero recognize that he or she has acted in error, and he lists several ways in which such recognition (*anagnorisis*) can take place. Some scholars, however, reject this as a fixed rule or criterion of correct tragic playwriting, and deny that there is a "master narrative" of tragedy. This is, I think, a view worth taking into consideration, for it avoids ruling out some of the extant plays as "lesser" tragedies or "not true tragedies."[3]

The case of reversal of fortune that Aristotle considers the best for poetic purposes is the fall from a state of great comfort and acclaim to a miserable condition, as exemplified in Sophocles' *Oedipus the King*. Such reversal of fortune elicits fear and sympathy in the audience. Fear, evidently, is achieved in Greek tragedy by means of the impending doom inherent in the tragic plot, which the audience knows in advance; there must have been suspense for Greek theatergoers in waiting for the ax to fall. Sympathy, in the sense that Aristotle is interested in, does not imply agreement or even intellectual tolerance of the actions of the tragic hero; it is rather an unavoidable solidarity with his or her suffering—a solidarity possibly stemming from the realization that what happened to the hero also could conceivably happen to the members of the audience.

As a natural result of fear and sympathy, tragedy produces a *katharsis* in the spectators, says Aristotle. The problem is that nobody really knows what that "catharsis" is. "Purification" is the literal meaning of the Greek word, but again etymology, as in other matters about Greek tragedy, is not very helpful. What does Aristotle mean? I don't believe that one can fully elucidate this question, but it seems clear that he implies a positive effect on the audience, very different from the negative one that Socrates talks about in the *Republic*. Perhaps "catharsis" means a feeling of liberation, after deriving a moral lesson from the suffering of the tragic hero, which has come about because of his/her hamartia. It is not hard to imagine the relief felt when, after witnessing the hero's realization of his own error and his downfall, the spectators return to their lives unscathed. The tragic events of the play did not befall any of them after all, they have enjoyed the artistry of the performance, and they have been given food for thought, or even improved their understanding of moral questions.

In addition to the formal requirements of the tragic play that we have seen above, there are a few others, some of which come from Aristotle, others that have been attributed to him rightly or wrongly. One is the unity of plot, the focus on one story, without subplots or distractions; another is the temporal unit, which requires the events of a tragedy to take place in a single day. Finally, we also find that the classical theory of tragedy maintained that the plot should move forward logically—that every action should succeed a previous one in manner that stands to reason, and that all the events of a tragedy should occur in the same location.

Aristotle's *Poetics* is a brief but very rich text, which can be read to great benefit by anyone interested in Greek tragedy or, indeed, dramatic writing of any kind. The preceding paragraphs are only a summary of the main points. Nevertheless, we must remember that Aristotle writes about an already long-standing tradition of poetry in general and tragedy in particular, out of which he selects the elements that he considers essential. Most of the poets had written without his guidance, and many great poets wrote later without special regard for it. This is as it should be, for theory can never substitute for the practice of an art. Consequently, it is to the poets and the plays that we must turn, first and last, if we really want to understand Greek tragedy.

SOPHOCLES

Aristotle considered Sophocles to be the best example of a tragic writer, and he judged *Oedipus the King*, the first of the plays in this volume, to be the best example of a tragedy. Whether this is deserved or not can, of course, be debated. Aristotle seems to have agreed with the majority view, for Sophocles was much more popular and respected than his contemporaries Aeschylus (525–456 B.C.) and Euripides (c.484–406).

Born around 497, he was not only a successful poet, but also held the position of treasurer of the Delian League (443–442) at the time that Athens was subjecting all the members of this league, under Athens' leadership, to the payment of tribute; he was also a general with Pericles in 441 and 440, and again from 426 to 423. In 413, at eighty-four years of age, he was named *proboulos*, one of the ten members of an emergency cabinet that was appointed immediately after the disaster of the Sicilian expedition in order to supplement the efforts of the ordinary political organs (the Council and the Assembly) in the conduct of the war against Sparta and its allies. The role of these ten people seems to have been short-lived, but it is clear that the men whom the Athenians appointed as *probouloi* must have been considered both truly wise and courageous, for this was Athens' most desperate hour.

When he died in 405, his life had nearly spanned the fifth century, which saw a number of important innovations in tragedy, mainly due to him: A third actor was introduced, allowing for one of the three to stand out as the tragic hero who will forge ahead to a fateful end; the number of chorus members increased to fifteen, divided in two halves under a chorus leader; and dialogue acquired much more relevance in the plays, substituting for lengthy messenger speeches and longer lyric parts. In addition, Sophocles wrote self-standing plays that could be understood without the need to have seen the other two plays in the trilogy. These innovations must have been appreciated by the public and made it easier to enjoy the performances and to understand their message. The writing of self-standing plays benefits us moderns too, since the only surviving tragic trilogy is Aeschylus' *Oresteia* (*Agamemnon*, *Libation-Bearers*, and *Eumenides*).

Sophocles' poetry achieved great popularity but was not of any lesser quality than that of his contemporaries. On the contrary, his tragedies are among the most powerful; in the original Greek, his verse is delightful, and is still used as a model for Greek verse composition by the few who study it. We cannot be entirely sure what classical Greek sounded like, but the actors probably delivered the lines spoken by Sophocles' characters with special ease.

We have seven extant plays by Sophocles, out of the more than 120 that he wrote, of which about thirty were produced and about twenty won first prize. The titles of the surviving ones are the following: *Electra*,[4] about the family the Atreidae; the *Trachiniae*, about Hercules; *Ajax* and *Philoctetes*, about the Trojan war; and the three included in this volume, about the family the Labdacidae (*Antigone*, *Oedipus the King*, and *Oedipus at Colonus*). We know enough about the dates of these last three plays to be sure that they did not form a trilogy: *Antigone* is the earliest one, produced in 441, *Oedipus the King* was produced around 429, and *Oedipus at Colonus* was written in 406 and 405 and produced posthumously in 401. Nevertheless, *Antigone* often is presented last of the three in modern editions for the sake of the overall continuity of the action.

Before looking into each of these three plays separately, a few words are in order about the background of the Labdacidae of Thebes. The family is named after Labdacus, a direct descendant of Cadmus, mythical founder of Thebes. Labdacus' son, Laius, becomes king of that city and marries Jocasta, also a descendant of Cadmus by a different line. Laius learns from the oracle of Delphi that his son will eventually kill him. At first, Laius avoids intercourse with Jocasta, but eventually she makes him drunk and takes him to bed, where she conceives their child. As soon as the boy is born, Laius pierces his feet with a nail, binds them, and exposes him on Mount Cithareon. The boy Oedipus (meaning "swollen foot") is rescued by a shepherd and raised in Corinth by King Polybus and his wife, Merope. Eventually Oedipus learns about the prophecy that he will kill his father and marry his mother. He flees Corinth and meets Laius on a narrow passage of the road to Delphi. Following a dispute between them, Oedipus kills Laius.

Oedipus marches on to Thebes, a city terrorized by the Sphinx, a winged lion with a woman's face sent by the goddess Hera in order to punish Thebes for the kidnapping of a boy. The Sphinx stops travelers and asks the following question: "What has four legs in the morning, two in the afternoon, and three in the evening?" Many have failed to answer correctly and have been devoured by the Sphinx, but Oedipus guesses the answer: "Man,"[5] he says, upon which the Sphinx hurls itself to its death from Mount Phicium. The Thebans acclaim Oedipus as a savior and make him their king. As such, he marries Jocasta, his own mother, thereby fulfilling the prophecy, polluting the city and putting a curse on their four children, born of incest: the boys Eteocles and Polynices, and the girls Antigone and Ismene. The story was one that the Greeks knew well. Even though Oedipus' true identity is unknown to the characters at the start of the play, the audience knows it, and everything about what will happen to him. In the remainder of this introduction, I have included plot summaries of the plays in order to enable readers to place themselves in the position of an "omniscient reader" if they so choose. Readers who prefer to discover the details of the story as they go along are advised to skip the last three sections of this introduction and return to them after reading the plays if they wish to learn about some of the main approaches to their interpretation.

Finally, one more remark can be made about Sophocles' choice of the story of the Labdacidae as the basis for some of his tragic plots: He may have tried to present mythical, evil-ridden Thebes as a foil for the democratic and flourishing Athenian society of the fifth century: Thebes is polluted by Oedipus' murder of his father, and its political rule is unstable, since Creon still has designs on its kingship that he will later put to effect in ways that are devastating for the city and his own family. At least part of the Athenian audience must have felt that, in contrast with Thebes, their city was definitely ruled in a just and stable manner.

OEDIPUS THE KING

At the opening of the play, Oedipus is asked by the Thebans to ease their suffering. The good years that followed Oedipus' arrival are behind, and again the city needs Oedipus to become its savior and free them from the blight that keeps their fields, their cattle, and their women barren. According to the oracle of Delphi, consulted by Creon, the blight is caused by the presence of the murderer of Laius in Thebes, and the remedy can be only the punishment of the murderer. Hoping to deliver Thebes from devastation a second time, Oedipus immediately starts an investigation.

Prophecy plays a very important role in the play, as it does in the Oedipus myth. This time, the blind prophet Tiresias will tell Oedipus that Oedipus himself is the killer. Oedipus cannot believe this to be true, and he accuses Jocasta's brother Creon of conspiracy; Creon asserts his innocence by means of a sacred oath. The investigation comes to a standstill, and Jocasta casts doubt on the prophecy, citing her belief that Laius' death did not come about in accordance with it. Oedipus enquires further, and he suspects that he might have been the killer. One key witness is mentioned by Jocasta: one of the heralds who accompanied Laius, a survivor from the attack, who reported that Laius had been killed by thieves (more than one) and then left Thebes to live as a shepherd. Oedipus sends for him in order to confirm such an exonerating report, since Oedipus was alone when he met with Laius on the road.

While Jocasta tries very hard to console Oedipus, even to the point of suggesting that incest is not the end of the world, a messenger arrives and announces that king Polybus is dead, and that the people of Corinth acclaim Oedipus as their new king. Oedipus also learns from the messenger that Polybus was not his real father. That same messenger delivered Oedipus as a baby to Polybus, after finding him on Mount Cithareon. They discuss the details of his bound feet and that another shepherd had carried him there following Laius' orders.

Jocasta fears that the truth now suspected by all may be uncovered and tries to call off the investigation, but Oedipus insists. The shepherd is brought in for questioning, and the truth is finally revealed, albeit with difficulty. Jocasta commits suicide, and Oedipus, ripping off the brooches that hold her clothes, buries them in his eye sockets. Oedipus, blinded, laments his fate and departs from Thebes into exile, forced to leave his children under Creon's custody.

The plot of *Oedipus the King* is so effective from the dramatic point of view that this play has dominated many (perhaps too many) debates about Greek tragedy. It has also prompted many interpretations that seek to elucidate the source of its strength. In *The Interpretation of Dreams*, Sigmund Freud applied his psychoanalytic theory to the analysis of the play and concluded that *Oedipus the King* reflects every man's innate desire to kill his own father and have sex with his own mother. Because psychoanalysis was a favored scientific discipline in the twentieth century, this analysis became quite popular. Today, however, most scholars acknowledge that the play breaks these two basic social taboos, but they place the emphasis of their research on other elements of the play that contribute to its success, such as the inexorably logical progression of the action.

What of the main character? When the idea of a "tragic flaw" (see the section "Tragic Errors and Their Realization," above) was in favor among theorists, Oedipus was seen as a character whose tragic flaw is his pride—a pride that compels him to attempt to escape his own fate. Today, however, we are not bound to interpret the play in this way. We can simply understand Oedipus' efforts at discovering the truth as misguided. His well-intentioned plan to save the city once again backfires because he cannot know that he himself is the murderer he is looking for.

Oedipus is loved by the Thebans, and Jocasta asks him to let the identity of Laius' murderer remain unknown. But Oedipus cannot. The play is clearly ominous from the very beginning, and its dramatic force derives from a contrast between the infallibility of divine knowledge, expressed in prophecy, and Oedipus' unquenchable thirst for knowledge of a past that will prove to be his own undoing. There is also a strong implication that true knowledge lies beyond what we can see. Blind Tiresias knows the truth, while Oedipus, who sees the light of day, knows only appearances and will lose his sight after he learns the whole truth about himself. With this ending, the play unequivocally reinforces the value of prophecy, which had come under attack in fifth-century Athens at the hands of the Sophists, who questioned this aspect of Greek traditional religion. Divine knowledge of the future thus prevails over the free will of an individual human being. This may seem hard to accept for a modern reader, but it probably did not seem so for an Athenian citizen, who probably had little or no concept of individual free will. On the contrary, religious practices and respect for the will of the gods emphasized social interaction and collective ritual, which was far preferable to single rule by a hero or by any more or less "enlightened" character. Just as the beloved Oedipus turns out not to benefit from his own pursuit of knowledge and fails to be the great ruler he seemed to be, there is no such thing as a good tyrant.

OEDIPUS AT COLONUS

After his departure from Thebes, Oedipus arrives at Colonus,[6] near Athens, with his daughter Antigone. Unknowingly, they enter the holy ground of the Eumenides, on which no one should tread. When they learn where they are from an Athenian citizen and he asks them to leave, Oedipus refuses, requests the presence of the Athenian king Theseus, and prays to the goddesses, requesting some consummation for his life, now that he has reached his final destination, according to prophecy. The chorus of citizens then asks him again to leave the forbidden grove; at first they promise him shelter, in view of his blindness and old age, but they later withdraw their offer when they find out who he is.

At different times in this play, Oedipus makes an elaborate apology for his past actions and current predicament: Man is helpless against fate, and exile came upon him after Creon first refused to bring death to him and then sent him away. Now, he says, he can help Athens greatly. Ismene arrives from Thebes with a report about the power struggle between the two brothers Polynices and Eteocles, and about the eventual success of the latter. Polynices has now enlisted help from Argos to march against his brother at Thebes. Further, Ismene reports the Thebans' intentions to retrieve Oedipus, since they also know of the prophecy that his buried corpse will bring victory to the people in whose land it rests.

But Oedipus has no plans to return. He is vengeful against both of his sons, who made him an exile and a fugitive, just as he is appreciative of his two daughters, who care for him so lovingly. Theseus arrives, and Oedipus informs him that one day Athens will be at war against Thebes, and that Athens will be successful if Oedipus is buried in Colonus. Theseus agrees to shelter him until his death. After Theseus' departure, Creon predictably arrives and tries to take Oedipus back to Thebes.

Creon at first expresses pity for Oedipus and his daughters, but Oedipus refuses to accompany him, for he knows that he will not really be taken back to Thebes, but instead will be buried just inside the border, to keep the city safe from Athens. Creon then uses force and sends first Ismene and then Antigone on their way back to Thebes.

Theseus returns with his guards. When he learns about the latest events, he prepares for the rescue of the two women and tells Creon that he is to remain in Athens until the women are returned. Creon speaks of Oedipus' past again, implying that he might bring pollution to Athens too, but Oedipus makes a long defense and explains that Athens is very respectful of the gods and will not suffer because of harboring him. Theseus marches away with Creon and succeeds in bringing back Antigone and Ismene.

Polynices then approaches. He explains his situation (already known to Oedipus from Ismene) and requests Oedipus' blessing for his upcoming expedition. Oedipus refuses, reminds Polynices of his failure to save him from exile, and prophesies that his two sons will die at each other's hands. Because he has already enlisted all his allies, Polynices has to march on to Thebes without his father's support. Anticipating disaster for himself, Polynices requests that Antigone bury him if he falls in combat.

At the sign of thunder, Oedipus knows that Zeus has come for him and requests Theseus' presence again. After telling Thesus that he is the only one to know where his body will lie, Oedipus takes leave from his daughters and goes away to a mysterious death, in which he seems to ascend to the company of the gods. Antigone and Ismene return to Thebes.

Oedipus at Colonus was produced posthumously around 401, following the defeat of Athens in the Peloponnesian War against Sparta and its allies. The audience of the play had witnessed the surrender of the legendary Athenian fleet, and the replacement of their cherished democratic institutions by the sinister rule of the Thirty Tyrants, appointed by the Spartans. Democracy did come back in 401, but Athens was never the same again. It is no wonder that Sophocles, who had written the play in 406 and 405, tried to nurture the Athenian patriotic spirit by means of a prophecy that *will* make Athens victorious in a future confrontation against Thebes, a city rife with crime, violence among relatives, and lies, as we saw in *Oedipus the King* and see again in this play.

The power of prophecy is also very important in this play, but now Oedipus has time to reflect on his fate and, as a result, deals with his guilt differently. He defends himself at length: He could not have known Laius' and his own real identities, and he killed Laius in self-defense, since Laius would have taken his life instead. Oedipus becomes, in fact, a hero with his own cult, like the many heroes who were actually celebrated in the Greek world of the fifth century. These heroes were often characters from Homer's *Iliad* (where the word *heros* simply means "warrior"), such as Achilles or Ajax, but they could also be men who became the object of a hero cult after their death, like the Spartan general Brasidas or, more important for us here, Sophocles himself, because he had hosted the statue of the god Asclepius when it was taken to Athens.[7]

The political situation and the hero cult are two important elements to bear in mind when reading this play. In addition, the play establishes continuity of the action between *Oedipus the King* and *Antigone*, and features a large number of entrances and exits, allowing for more interaction between characters on stage than in previous pieces. In the end, Oedipus seems strangely to come to terms with his own life; he no longer has regrets, nor does he ask for favors from gods or humans. He seems to place his faith in the gods unconditionally, in the knowledge, as he says, that "it is only for the gods that there is no old age or death: the rest is effaced by all-powerful Time. The strength of the land will decay and the strength in man's body will decay, but loyalty too will perish and disloyalty thrive. The same spirit does not endure between men who are friends, or between one city and another."[8]

ANTIGONE

The action of Antigone begins after the battle in which Polynices and his six allies, who have attacked Thebes in an attempt to wrestle power from Eteocles, have been defeated, and Eteocles has also died in the confrontation.[9] Creon, who now finds himself ruler of Thebes, seeks to make an example of Polynices by leaving his body unburied so that wild beasts will devour it. Antigone, who is to be married to Creon's son

Haemon, will not allow Creon's orders to stand. She buries (and reburies) her brother's corpse, incurring Creon's wrath. Her penalty—one that Creon had instituted against whoever ignored his command—is to be taken away to die of starvation in an underground prison. Haemon intervenes and asks his father to reconsider. Eventually Creon accedes to Haemon's request, and they depart toward Antigone's prison. But it is too late: Antigone has hung herself. Haemon then dies by his own sword, next to her. In grief, his mother, Eurydice, also kills herself. Creon is left alone, lamenting the loss of his son, wife, and niece. A loss caused by fate, he says.

The ritual of burial was extremely important in Greek religion, and Antigone's insistence on it under the circumstances of the play would not have seemed out of place at all to a Greek audience. Overwhelmingly, the core of the play has been understood to be the conflict between the individual and the state, which is brought about by the direct confrontation between a personal moral imperative derived from traditional belief and the laws of the city. This interpretation is mostly correct, although it is important to stay clear of two common interpretive mistakes that are often associated with it: First, it is not obvious that the play takes Antigone's side, at least before her own life is actually put in the balance. Initially, the play is sympathetic to Creon as the upholder of public order, and the language suggests that Antigone's deviant behavior, her honoring a potential destroyer of the city, should not be tolerated. Second, there is no clear opposition between the "unwritten" laws of the gods that Antigone follows and any laws "written" by Creon, because the original Greek does not contain such a sharp antithesis. What we have is a contrast between the unwritten precepts (*nomima*) of the gods and Creon's proclamations (*kerugmata*). Legal terminology is still imprecise at this stage of Greek history, but something else is also at play: This is Thebes, not Athens, and the question does not come down squarely on the possible conflict between sacred laws and the laws of the people (the people were not an agent in Thebes). Nevertheless, there is an undeniable tension between individual and collective interests in a broad sense, and the play seems to ask a pressing question about how far legislative activity can go—at a time when the Athenians were busy elaborating a legal system for their city.

Last, but not least, there is of course the gender-based conflict between female Antigone and male Creon, which Sophocles does not forget to underscore by making Creon declare that he will not be ruled by a woman. The question is: Was that statement meant to elicit the sympathy of an Athenian audience for Antigone, or for Creon? The answer to that question has a direct bearing on the answer to a related one: Who is the tragic hero in *Antigone*? Antigone breaks the law while she believes that she is only honoring her brother according to sacred tradition, and she pays for her error with her life. Creon, on the other hand, seeks only to uphold the law in his own city, but his actions are ultimately responsible for the death of three members of his family.

Part of the difficulty in answering these questions stems from the fact that the production of *Antigone* pre-dates that of *Oedipus the King*, and therefore the notion of a main tragic character may well not have yet developed. Clearly, however, later audiences have sided and continue to side with Antigone, perhaps because she has come to represent individual freedom of thought and conscience, a notion cherished by modern democratic societies, and a notion that seems ever threatened by the arbitrary exercise of power. Political ideas may differ and require extensive discursive confrontation in order to determine the right course of action, but the discourse must never be interrupted by force. This is, I believe, what continues to give *Antigone* its emblematic character.

—Inwood, Manhattan
August 2006

Pedro de Blas holds degrees in law and classics and has taught Greek at Columbia University and at the CUNY Latin/Greek Institute. He has acted in several productions of Greek tragedy in the original. He is the author of the introduction and notes to *Essential Dialogues of Plato*, also published by Barnes & Noble Classics.

ACKNOWLEDGMENTS

Writing an introduction and notes on Sophoclean tragedy aimed at the general reader requires the knowledge and the sort of perspective that I could not manage alone. I would like to thank my dear Silvia for commenting on successive drafts over a long summer, and both Jeffrey Broesche and George Stade for their editing and book production efforts.

NOTES

1. In the remainder of this introduction, all dates are B.C.E. unless otherwise specified or self-evident.
2. Here I follow H. Epps' helpful note 18 in Aristotle, *Poetics*, translated by H. Epps, Chapel Hill: University of North Carolina Press, 1942, p. 24.
3. P. Burian, "Myth into *Muthos*: The Shaping of Tragic Plot," in *The Cambridge Companion to Greek Tragedy*, edited by P. E. Easterling, Cambridge: Cambridge University Press, 1997, p. 181.
4. Not to be confused with Euripides' play of the same title and subject.
5. Man crawls on all fours as an infant, later walks on two feet, and uses a walking stick in old age.
6. Reputed to be Sophocles' place of birth.
7. B. Knox, "Introduction," in *Sophocles: The Three Theban Plays*, translated by R. Fagles, New York: Penguin Classics, 2000, p. 257.
8. Lines 570–576 in the translation.
9. This confrontation had been the subject of Aeschylus' tragedy *Seven Against Thebes*.

NOTE ON THE TRANSLATOR

Peter Constantine's most recent translations are *The Essential Writings of Machiavelli* (Modern Library, 2007) and *The Bird is a Raven* by Benjamin Lebert (Knopf, 2006), which was awarded the Helen and Kurt Wolff Translation Prize. He was awarded the PEN Translation Prize for *Six Early Stories by Thomas Mann*, and the National Translation Award for *The Undiscovered Chekhov—Thirty-Eight New Stories*. His translation of the complete works of Isaac Babel received the Koret Jewish Literature Award and a National Jewish Book Award citation. He has recently translated *Within Four Walls: The Correspondence between Hannah Arendt and Heinrich Blücher, 1936–1968* for Harcourt, and Gogol's *Taras Bulba*, Tolstoy's *The Cossacks*, and Voltaire's *Candide* for Modern Library.

Peter Constantine was one of the editors for *A Century of Greek Poetry: 1900–2000*, and is currently co-editing an anthology of Greek poetry since Homer for W.W. Norton. His translation of Stylianos Harkianakis' poetry collection, *Mother*, received the Hellenic Association of Translators of Literature Prize. He is a senior editor of *Conjunctions* and lives in New York.

ACKNOWLEDGMENTS

I would like to thank Columbia University's libraries for making available their extensive collection of classical material, which was a great help in translating these plays. I am especially thankful to Karen Green, the Librarian of Ancient and Medieval History and Religion.

I am grateful to Rachel Hadas for her insights and understanding of Sophocles' poetry. I would also like to thank Karen Van Dyck for her advice and support, and Vayos Liapis for elucidating some of the complexities of Sophoclean language.

My gratitude also to Roger Celestin for his advice and editorial help, to Jeffrey Broesche, my editor at Barnes & Noble Classics, and to Burton Pike for his encouragement and support.

OEDIPUS THE KING

CHARACTERS

OEDIPUS	king of Thebes
PRIEST	of Zeus
CREON	brother of Jocasta
CHORUS	of Theban citizens
TIRESIAS	a blind prophet
JOCASTA	the queen, widow of Laius and married to Oedipus
A MESSENGER	from Corinth
A SHEPHERD	former servant of Laius
A SECOND MESSENGER	from inside the palace

Non-speaking

Suppliants

Tiresias' Guide

Palace Attendants

Antigone and Ismene
daughters of Oedipus and Jocasta

[In front of OEDIPUS' palace in Thebes.
Enter OEDIPUS with attendants.]

OEDIPUS

My children, newest offspring of ancient Thebes,
why do you gather here before me
with the garlanded branches of suppliants,[1]
the city's air heavy with incense,
despairing chants and lamentation?
I did not want to hear your words
from messengers, so I myself have come,
illustrious Oedipus, known to all.

[To the PRIEST]

Revered old man, tell me, since it is fitting
that you speak for all, how you have come here—
in fear or in hope? I will help you
in every way. I would be hard-hearted if
I did not feel compassion for your plight.

PRIEST

Oedipus, ruler of our land! We are here
gathered at your altars, some not yet able
to spread their wings, others weighed down by age.
I am the Priest of Zeus. These boys
have been chosen from among unmarried youths,
and that throng, decked with garlands,
has gathered near Athena's two temples
and by Apollo Ismenius' oracular ashes.
You yourself see how the city is pitching and tossing,
Unable to raise its head from the murderous depths!
Withering are the buds that bear the fruits of earth,
withering the cattle in the pastures, withering
the unborn seed in our women's wombs.
The fire-bearing god, abhorrent Pestilence,
has descended on the city of Thebes,

emptying the House of Cadmus,*
and black Hades† grows rich as we lament our dead.
It is not because we revere you as a deity
that we have gathered by your altars,
but because you are first among men,
wise in the ways of mortals and of gods.
You freed our city from its deadly tribute
to the Sphinx,‡ that cruel enchantress,
without knowledge or instruction from us,
but, as we believe, with the help of a god.
We know that you set our lives aright.
But now, great and mighty Oedipus,
we beg you to protect us once again,
deliver us with help of god or man.
For your experience and trials in past strife
give strength to your present counsel.
First among men, rebuild this city! All of Thebes
calls you its savior for your former deeds.
Take care for your name! Let us not remember
that in the beginning you raised us up
only later to watch us fall.
Keep us from falling! Raise Thebes once again!
Auspicious was the omen
with which you gave us good fortune.
—Do the same once more!
You are our king, but is it not better
to rule a land of the living than a land of desolation?
An empty tower and an empty ship are worthless
unless filled with men.

---

*Founder of Thebes.

†God of the underworld.

‡Winged lion with the face of a woman that had terrorized Thebes before Oedipus' arrival (see Introduction).

OEDIPUS

Poor children! I know the plight with which you come to me.
I know that you are beset, but none of you are as beset as I.
Your suffering comes to each of you alone,
to yourself, to no other. But my soul
laments for this city, for myself, and for you.
You did not wake me from a sweet slumber.
Know that I have shed many tears
and wandered down many paths of thought.
I have undertaken the one redress I came upon.
I have sent the son of Menoeceus, Creon, my own brother-in-law,
to Delphi,* to the Pythian halls of Apollo,† to hear from the god
what I should do or say to save the city.
I have been counting the days, and am already worried
that he has stayed away so long. But when he returns,
I would be the worst of men if I did not do all that Apollo decrees.

PRIEST

Your words are timely. Those men
are signaling that Creon has returned.

OEDIPUS

O Lord Apollo! May he come
as a shining savior in good fortune.

PRIEST

The news must be good, or Creon's head
would not be richly crowned with laurels.

---

*Location of the most famous oracle in ancient Greece.

†God of prophecy.

OEDIPUS

We will know soon, he is close enough to hear.

[Enter CREON]

Lord Creon, son of Menoeceus, dear kinsman!
What prophetic words of Apollo do you bring?

CREON

Good words! For I believe that even what is hard to bear,
if it turns out well, can lead to good fortune.

OEDIPUS

What message do you bring? Your words
do not alarm me, but they do not give me hope.

CREON

Shall I report in the presence of these people?
I am ready to speak here, or follow you inside.

OEDIPUS

Speak out to all. I lament for my people[2]
more than for myself.

CREON

Then I will tell you what I heard from the god.
Shining Apollo commands us to cleanse a stain from our land,
a stain congealed within Thebes, to stop nurturing it
in our city, to drive it out.

OEDIPUS

What cleansing? What is the nature of this stain?

CREON

We must banish a man, or repay murder with murder:
for it is spilt blood that is blighting Thebes.

OEDIPUS

Who is the man whose fate Apollo reveals?

CREON

Laius once ruled this land, King Oedipus,
before you took over this city's helm.

OEDIPUS

I have heard that, though it was before I came.

CREON

He was killed, and Apollo tells us to raise our hands
to punish his murderers, whoever they may be.

OEDIPUS

But where are these murderers? Where can we find
the trail of such a distant crime?

CREON

In our own city, Apollo said. What you will hunt
you will capture, and what you neglect will escape.

OEDIPUS

Was Laius murdered here, in his house,
in his field, or in some faraway land?

CREON

He set out for the Oracle at Delphi, as he told us,
but did not return from the journey.

OEDIPUS

Could no attendant or escort
tell us something that could help?

CREON

All his attendants were killed, except for one man
who ran away in terror, and reported only a single thing.

OEDIPUS

What was it? A single thing
can be a key to many things.

CREON

He said that robbers attacked, that King Laius
did not die by one man's hand, but at the hands of many.

OEDIPUS

What robber would have dared this deed, unless
he had been bribed perhaps by Theban silver?

CREON

That is what all believe. But after Laius' end
no one came to aid us in our strife.

OEDIPUS

When disaster strikes a throne, what strife
can hinder you from seeking the culprits?

CREON

The Sphinx singing her deadly riddles[3]
turned our eyes from all but what lay at hand.

OEDIPUS

I shall shed light on everything. Apollo is right,
and so are you, to turn your attention to the murdered king.
You shall see me fighting justly at your side to aid this city,
with Apollo's help. I shall dispel this pollution—
not on behalf of a distant friend but for my own sake:
whoever killed King Laius may well raise his hand
to harm me. By defending him I defend myself.
Come, children, rise from these altars,
and take away the suppliants' branches.

[To an attendant]

Call together the people of Thebes, and tell them
that I shall do whatever need be done!
Either we shall prevail with Apollo's help,
or we shall fall!

[OEDIPUS, CREON, and attendants exit into the palace]

PRIEST

Let us rise, my children. Oedipus proclaims
of his own accord the favor for which we came.
May Apollo, who has sent these oracles, come to us
as a savior and end the plague.

*[The PRIEST and the suppliants leave.
Enter the CHORUS of Theban elders.]*

CHORUS

Sweet sounding voice of Zeus,
what message
do you bring to resplendent Thebes
from gold-gifted Delphi?
I am racked,
my heart trembles. Quivering in terror I call out to you,
Apollo, Healer of Delos,*
I stand in dread before you.
What debt will you demand from us—one that is new,
or one that recurs with the cycle of seasons?
Tell me, offspring of golden hope, immortal and divine voice!

First I call to you, Daughter of Zeus,
immortal Athena,
I call on your sister Artemis,
protectress of our land, seated
upon her glorious round throne
above our market square.
I call on far-casting† Apollo!
O appear before me, you gods,
threefold shield against death!

---

*Apollo, born on the island of Delos, is also the god of healing.

†Apollo is often called "far-casting" or "far-shooting" because his arrows travel far.

If ever you have come
to banish beyond our borders the flames of calamity
springing up within our city,
come now again!

O countless are the woes that I must bear!
Our entire city is beset by plague,
nor have we spears of mind to ward it off.
The fruits of our glorious earth do not grow,
nor are our women and the infants alive
in the silence that follows the shrieks of childbirth.
One after the other you see those who still live,
like swift-winged birds, pass faster
than a raging fire to the shores of Hades.

With such myriad deaths the city perishes.
Unlamented and unpitied her sons lie upon the earth
in death-spreading pestilence,
while wives and grayhaired mothers
crowding around the altar
wail out their baneful pain.
Voices gasp, and songs ring forth
to Apollo the Healer.
Golden daughter of Zeus, send us
the shining countenance of help.

Raging Ares,* though now
without his bronze shield of war,
wraps me in flames and shrieking death:
grant that he turn in rapid flight from our city,
thrust by a favorable wind

*God of war.

far into the great chamber of Amphitrite's* ocean
or the inhospitable Thracian sea,
for whatever raging torment
the night leaves undone,
the day will accomplish.
Zeus our Father, wielder
of flame-bearing lightning,
destroy Ares with your thunderbolt.

Apollo, Lycian Lord,
let the invincible arrows
of your gold-twined bowstring
shower forth in our defense,
like the fiery flash of Artemis' torches
as she darts through the Mountains of Lycia.
I call upon Bacchus,† the golden-wreathed god
who gave Bacchic Thebes its name,
wine-flushed Bacchus,
companion of the Maenads:‡
with your flaming pine torch
come to our aid
against Ares, the god dishonored among gods.

[OEDIPUS enters from the palace]

OEDIPUS

You are praying. Your prayers will be granted
if you hear my words obediently
and are prepared to do what this disease requires.
I, a stranger to this matter, a stranger to the murderous deed,
shall speak out. Were I to seek the truth alone,

---

*Amphitrite is the wife of Poseidon, god of the sea.

†A.k.a. Dionysos. See Introduction for more on Dionysos.

‡Women who celebrate Dionysos with frantic sound and dance.

I could not go far without any signs.
It was only after the deed that I became
a Theban among Thebans.
Hence I proclaim this to all you descendants of Cadmus:
I command that what man among you
knows who killed Laius, son of Labdakos,
reveal all to me. And should this man be afraid
of admitting to the deed, I assure him that no harm
will come to him. He will be sent from this land in safety.
And if someone knows that the murderer is another man,
or a man from another land, then he must speak out.
I shall reward him and he will have my gratitude as well.
But if whoever knows keeps silent, thrusting aside my words,
either fearing for a friend or for himself, then hear what I shall do:
I shall prohibit any man of this land
in which I hold the power and the throne,
to receive him, address a word to him,
perform a prayer or sacrifice with him,
or share with him the lustral water.
He will be denied all men's houses,
for he is the polluting stain, as the god's Delphic oracle
has so clearly revealed to me.
Such an ally shall I be to the god
and to the murdered man.
I pray most earnestly that the slayer,
whether the deed was done unnoticed
or in the company of others, will find
his wretched life withering in the most vile misery.
I also pray that if I ever let him share my hearth and home,
then may I suffer the same fate I have just decreed.
I order you to discharge these commands most scrupulously,
for my sake, for the sake of the god, and for the sake of our land
destroyed and barren, abandoned by the gods.

For even if this were not sent by the gods,
you could not have left it uncleansed— 252
the slain man was the best of men, your king—
it should have been searched out. More so now
that I hold the power he held before,
sowing the same marriage bed and wife. 256
He and I would have generated
common sons from a common womb
if ill fortune had not descended upon his offspring.
But Fate did descend upon his head. 260
Therefore I shall fight on his behalf as if he were my father.
I shall leave nothing untried in my quest to find the man
who murdered the son of Labdakos, son of Polydoros,*
of the line of Cadmus and ancient Agenor.† 264
To those who do not do as I say, I pray that the gods
will allow no crops to rise from fields they have ploughed,
nor children from their women, but that they wither
under our city's present fate, or a fate more hateful. 268
As for all you other men of Thebes, who approve of my words:
may Justice, our ally, and the gods, forever give you grace.

CHORUS

My Lord, I shall say this, since you adjured me under a curse:
I did not slay Laius, nor can I point to the slayer. 272
It falls to Apollo, who sent us to search out this matter,
to tell us who committed the deed.

OEDIPUS

You are right. But no man can force the gods to do
what they do not want to do. 276

CHORUS

Then I would like to suggest what might be second best.

---

*Son of Cadmus.

†Mythical son of Poseidon, and father of Cadmus and Europa.

OEDIPUS

And if there is a third, do not omit to point it out.

CHORUS

I know that Lord Tiresias sees the future just as Lord Apollo does.
Looking into this matter with his help, Lord Oedipus,
you will learn the truth most clearly.

OEDIPUS

I have not delayed: at Creon's suggestion
I sent messengers twice to find Tiresias,
and wonder that he is still not here.

CHORUS

There are also some other tales that are vague and old.

OEDIPUS

What are they? I want to look into everything.

CHORUS

Laius was said to have been killed by wayfarers.

OEDIPUS

I have heard that too. But nobody has seen a man who saw the deed.

CHORUS

But if there is a culprit and he is susceptible to fear,
he will not resist once he hears the curses you pronounced.

OEDIPUS

He who did not fear the deed will hardly fear my words.

CHORUS

But there is one who will convict the slayer: here—
they are bringing the divine prophet in whom truth is implanted
above all other men.

[Enter TIRESIAS led by a youth]

OEDIPUS

Tiresias, you who discern everything, the clear and the hidden,
what is in heaven and what trods the earth.
Though you cannot see our city,
you understand the plague that has beset it.
In you, Lord Tiresias, we find our sole protector, our savior.
Apollo has given us an answer—as I am sure you have heard
from the messengers—to the question that we sent him:
we will only be released from this plague
if we relentlessly seek out the slayers of Laius,
and kill them or send them forth in banishment from this land.
Do not refuse us the oracular voice of birds
or any other path of divination that you have.
Save yourself and Thebes, save me, save all from the taint of guilt
that rises from the dead: we place ourselves in your hands.
The finest task is for a man to help with all his abilities and powers.

TIRESIAS

Woe! Woe! How terrible to have knowledge
that does not benefit the knower. I knew that well enough
but pushed it aside, otherwise I would not have come.

OEDIPUS

What do you mean? I see you have come faint of heart.

TIRESIAS

Let me go home. If you do so,
you will bear your burden better, and so shall I.

OEDIPUS

Your words rebuff the laws. If in face of the oracle
you withhold your response
you will prove yourself hostile to this city that nurtured you.

TIRESIAS

I see that you miss the point, and I do not want the same to happen to me.

OEDIPUS

By all the gods, if you have knowledge, do not turn away!
We all bow before you as suppliants.

TIRESIAS

You do so because you are foolish.
But I shall not reveal either my grief or yours.

OEDIPUS

What! You know but will not speak? You intend
to betray us and destroy Thebes?

TIRESIAS

I will not grieve myself or you. Why question me
to no avail? You will learn nothing from me.

OEDIPUS

No? O most evil of evil villains! You could rouse a rock to anger!
You will not speak out, but prove hard and obstinate?

TIRESIAS

You censure my wrath, but do not see
the wrath that lives with you. Instead you blame me.

OEDIPUS

Who would not become wrathful at hearing such words that dishonor Thebes.

TIRESIAS

All will emerge, even if I cloak it in silence.

OEDIPUS

If all will emerge, then why not tell me?

TIRESIAS

I shall say no more. Unleash, if you will, your raging anger upon me.

OEDIPUS

Then angered as I am, I shall leave nothing unsaid 336
of what I have understood. Know that I believe
you took part in contriving the deed and carrying it out,
even if you did not kill Laius with your own hands.
If you had sight, I would say that the deed was yours alone. 340

TIRESIAS

Really? Then I tell you to abide by the proclamation you just made,
and from this day forth address neither those present nor myself,
for you yourself are the profane polluter of this land.

OEDIPUS

What shameless tales are you unleashing? 344
How do you expect to escape the consequences?

TIRESIAS

I have escaped them, for within me I nurture the power of truth.

OEDIPUS

From whom did you learn this truth? It was hardly from your prophetic craft.

TIRESIAS

I learnt it from you. It was you who urged me to speak against my will. 348

OEDIPUS

And what was it you said? Say it again so that I can truly understand.

TIRESIAS

Have you really not understood?
Or are you pressing me to say it in a different way?

OEDIPUS

I cannot say that I understand your words. Speak them again. 352

TIRESIAS

I say that you are the murderer you are seeking.

OEDIPUS

You shall repent voicing disaster twice.

TIRESIAS

Shall I tell you something else that will anger you even more?

OEDIPUS

Say as much as you like: it will be in vain. 356

TIRESIAS

I will tell you that unknown to you, you are living in the greatest shame
with those closest to you, unable to see the evil in which you are immersed.

OEDIPUS

How do you think you can say such things unscathed?

TIRESIAS

I can if indeed there is power in truth. 360

OEDIPUS

There is, for all but you. For you there is not,
since your ears, your mind, and your eyes are blind.

TIRESIAS

You poor wretch, hurling the taunts at me
that all men will soon hurl at you. 364

OEDIPUS

You have been nourished by constant night.
You cannot harm me or any other seeing man.

TIRESIAS

It is not your fate to fall through me. Apollo can
and intends to bring it about.

OEDIPUS

Whose inventions are these? Creon's?[4]

TIRESIAS

Creon is no bane to you. You yourself are.

OEDIPUS

O wealth and kingship! O skill surpassing skill
in a life much envied! How great is the resentment
stored within you! It is for the sake of this rule
which the city placed in my hands, a gift unasked for,
that loyal Creon, a friend from the first,
has treacherously crept up on me, seeking to depose me.
He engaged this conjuror, this weaver of contrivances,
this treacherous beggar, who can see quite clearly
when there is profit, but is blind in his prophetic craft.
Come, tell me, how are you a true seer?
Why, when the rhapsodic Sphinx was here
did you not speak a word to free the Thebans from her thrall?
Her riddle was not to be unraveled by the first comer
but needed prophecy, which you were not seen to have,
neither from bird nor god. Then I came, Oedipus,
who knew nothing, and put an end to the Sphinx,
by wit, not by augury of birds. I am the one
you are now trying to depose, thinking you can draw close
to Creon's throne. You and he, who hatched this plot,
will weep at your zeal to drive out this curse.
If I did not think you too old, you would learn through suffering
the danger of your thoughts.

CHORUS

It seems to us that both Tiresias' words and yours, Oedipus,
are spoken in anger. We do not need such things,
but need to seek a way to solve the oracle of the god.

TIRESIAS

Though you rule as king, I claim 396
an equal right to counter your words.
I have this power because I do not live as your slave
but as the slave of Apollo; nor need I, a citizen of Thebes,
submit myself to Creon's patronage. And I shall say this, 400
since you have reproached me for being blind:
though you see clearly, you cannot see the evil you are in,
nor where and with whom you are dwelling.
Do you even know your provenance? 404
You are unaware that you are the enemy of your kin
both beneath and above the earth, unaware
that the double-edged curse of your mother and father
will one day fiercely drive you from this land in darkness, 408
though now your eyes can see. What place
will not be a haven to your cries,
from what part of Mount Cithaeron* will your cries not echo
when you realize what nuptials you sailed into, 412
sped by fate's favorable wind, your house a havenless haven.
And there are myriad other troubles of which you are not even
aware,
which will make you equal to your children.
So fling mud at Creon, fling mud at my words, 416
for there is no mortal who shall be crushed
more cruelly than you.

OEDIPUS

Am I to tolerate such words from this man?

---

*Mountain near Thebes.

Go to your ruin! Away with you!
Leave this house! Go back where you came from!

TIRESIAS

I would not be here if you had not called me.

OEDIPUS

I did not know that you would speak like such a fool,
or I would not have summoned you to my house.

TIRESIAS

I was born a fool, just as you say,
but the parents who bore you thought me wise.

OEDIPUS

What parents? What mortals bore me?

TIRESIAS

This day will give birth to you as well as destroy you.

OEDIPUS

Everything you say is so riddling and obscure!

TIRESIAS

Are you not a master at solving riddles?

OEDIPUS

You taunt me for what proved me a master.

TIRESIAS

But it was just this mastery that has proved your ruin.

OEDIPUS

As I saved the city, I do not care.

TIRESIAS

Well, I shall go. Boy, take me away.

OEDIPUS

Yes, take him from here.
Present, you are nothing but a hindrance.

Go, so that you will vex me no more.

TIRESIAS

I shall go when I have said what I was summoned for.
I shall do so without fear of your person, for you cannot
destroy me.
I say to you: the man you have been seeking for so long
with threats and proclamations, the murderer of Laius,
that man is here, thought to be a foreigner living among us.
But soon he will be revealed as Theban born,
a thing that will bring him no delight.
He will be blind, though now he can see,
poor though now he is rich; he will wander in foreign lands,
tapping the ground before him with a staff,
revealed as both brother and father to his children,
both husband and son to his mother,
and to his father fellow-sower in the marital bed and slayer.
Go into your house and weigh my words,
and if you find that I am wrong,
consider me as having no skill in prophecy.

[Exit TIRESIAS led by a youth]

CHORUS

Who is the man whom
the divine oracular rock at Delphi
proclaimed doer of this unspeakable deed
of murderous hand?
It is time that his feet
move faster in flight
than storm-swift horses,
for the son of Zeus leaps upon him
with fire and lightning,
and the dire Spirits of Death
that never miss their mark
are close at heel.

A voice has issued forth
from the snowy heights of Parnassus,
that all must follow the track
of this unknown man.
He roams through wild forests
like a bull, among caves and rocks,
wretchedly limping with wretched foot,
struggling to elude the oracles
rising from the navel of earth.
But the oracles are always alive,
hovering around him.

How dire, how very dire is the confusion
unleashed by the wise bird-augurer Tiresias.
I can neither accept his words nor reject them.
I know not what to say. I hover in hope,
unable to see the present,
or see what lies ahead.
I have not learned, before or now,
of strife between the House of Laius
and the son of Polybus,*
but nothing I know
could lead me to attack Oedipus,
glorious among the people,
and so aid the House of Laius
with this mysterious death.

Zeus and Apollo are wise and know the affairs of mortals,
but the judgment is mistaken that among men
a prophet is worth more than I.
One wisdom can surpass another.

*King of Corinth who raised Oedipus as his son.

But before I can be certain
that what was said is true,
I shall never side with those who blame Oedipus.
The winged Sphinx descended upon him
before all eyes,
and he proved himself wise
and a friend to our city.
Therefore in my mind I shall never
charge him with evil.

[Enter CREON]

CREON

Men of Thebes, I come here after hearing accusations
I cannot bear, dire accusations leveled at me by King Oedipus.
If in the present circumstances he believes
that he has suffered injury through any of my words or deeds,
then I do not wish for long life, bearing such hurt.
Nor is the damage of his words slight; it is most grievous
to be called evil, not only in the city, but by you and by my loved ones.

CHORUS

That charge must have come from the violence of anger
rather than considered judgment.

CREON

Did he not say that through my schemes
the prophet was swayed to speak false words?

CHORUS

These things were said, but I do not know
what thoughts prompted them.

CREON

Did he make this accusation against me
with steady eye and steady mind?

CHORUS

I do not know. I do not understand
the actions of the powerful.
But here is Oedipus, emerging from the palace.

OEDIPUS

You! How dare you come here?
You have the effrontery to come to my house,
you, the murderer of its master,
and before all eyes the thief of my kingship?
Tell me, by the gods, did you see in me cowardice
or foolishness that resolved you to do this?
Or did you think I would not notice your deed
creeping up on me, so that, unaware of it,
I could not protect myself?
But is not your undertaking foolish,
hunting without wealth and allies for a kingdom
that can only be captured with riches and the populace?

CREON

You must listen in turn to my answer,
and then judge for yourself what you will learn.

OEDIPUS

You are clever in speech, but I will prove bad at learning
from you,
as I have found you hard and hostile toward me.

CREON

Just for this reason, listen first to what I have to say.

OEDIPUS

Just for this reason, don't tell me you are not evil.

CREON

If you believe that senseless obstinacy is a worthy thing to
have,
then you are not thinking well.

OEDIPUS

If you believe you can do ill to a kinsman without suffering the penalty,
then you are not thinking well.

CREON

I agree that what you say is just. 544
But tell me what you say I did to you.

OEDIPUS

Did you or did you not persuade me
to send for the revered prophet?

CREON

I still stand by that counsel. 548

OEDIPUS

How long is it now that Laius—

CREON

I do not understand. That Laius did what?

OEDIPUS

—that Laius disappeared through that deadly, violent deed.

CREON

You would have to count years long and old. 552

OEDIPUS

And did the prophet in those days practice his craft?

CREON

He was as wise and honored as he is now.

OEDIPUS

Did he mention me at all during that time?

CREON

Not in my presence. 556

OEDIPUS

So you did not seek out the killer?

CREON

Of course we did. But we found nothing.

OEDIPUS

How is it that the wise man did not speak out?

CREON

I do not know. When I do not understand a thing, I keep my
silence. 560

OEDIPUS

But this thing you know and you could tell me,
since I am sure you understand it well.

CREON

What thing? If I know, I will not refuse to answer.

OEDIPUS

That if the soothsayer had not been in league with you, 564
he would not have attributed the death of Laius to me.

CREON

You know if that is what he said, not I.
But I claim the right to ask you questions, as you did just now.

OEDIPUS

Ask. For I shall not be found the murderer. 568

CREON

Well then, do you have my sister as your wife?

OEDIPUS

It would be impossible to say no.

CREON

Do you reign over this land with her as equal at your side?

OEDIPUS

She has from me whatever she might want.

CREON

And am I not, to the two of you, an equal third?

OEDIPUS

Which is precisely why you have shown yourself such an evil friend!

CREON

Not if you weigh my circumstance as I do. First, consider this:
do you believe a man would prefer to reign in constant fear
rather than hold the same power but sleep soundly?
Like any rational man, I am not one who would prefer
to be king rather than wield the power of a king. I have from you
everything I want without fear, but were I to reign,
I would have to do many things against my will. So why would I prefer
the burden of kingship to power and authority free from worry?
I am not so misguided that I would yearn for more than the honors
and advantages I already enjoy. Now all wish me well,
now all greet me kindly, now those who need something from you
call on me. Their success depends on me. Why should I prefer
your position to mine? A mind that is sound cannot turn to evil.
I do not admire that evil way of thinking, nor would I ever act in league
with anyone who did. As proof of this, go to Delphi and inquire
if I reported the oracle to you correctly. And if you find

that I plotted with the soothsayer, send me to my death,
not with just one vote, but two—yours and my own.
But do not accuse me on mere conjecture with no evidence.
It is as unjust to judge bad men good without cause
as it is to judge good men bad. Casting out a friend
is like casting out one's own life, which one loves so much.
But I am certain you will see this for yourself,
since time alone points to the just man,
while he who is evil can be exposed in a day.

CHORUS

He spoke well for one who is wary of falling, Lord.
Those who are fast in thinking are not surefooted.

OEDIPUS

When a conspirator moves quickly and stealthily,
I too must think quickly. If I wait calmly,
his deeds will be done, while mine will come to nothing.

CREON

What do you want? To banish me from this land?

OEDIPUS

No. I want your death, not your banishment.

[Lines missing in the Greek text]

CREON

When you have explained what envy you mean.

[Lines missing in the Greek text]

OEDIPUS

Do you mean you will not believe my words and yield?

CREON

I will not, for I see you are not reasoning well.

OEDIPUS

I am reasoning well from my position.

CREON

But you should also reason well from mine.

OEDIPUS

But you are evil!

CREON

You understand nothing.

OEDIPUS

But you must bow to my rule.

CREON

Not if you rule badly.

OEDIPUS

O Thebes! Thebes!

CREON

Thebes is my city too, not yours alone.

CHORUS

Cease, my lords. I see Jocasta emerging from the palace,
just in time. With her help this quarrel must be brought to an end.

[Enter JOCASTA]

JOCASTA

Why have you sparked this foolish battle of tongues,
you wretches? Are you not ashamed
to stir up private strife when our land is beset by plague?

[To OEDIPUS]

Go back inside, and you, Creon, to your house!
You cannot turn this trifling matter into something great.[5]

CREON

My sister! Your husband Oedipus sees it as just
to choose between two evils, either banishing me

from my native Thebes, or having me killed.

OEDIPUS

That is so. I have caught him, Jocasta, attempting 628
to do evil against me through evil schemes.

CREON

May I never prosper, and may I die under a curse
if I have done any of the things you say.

JOCASTA

By the gods, Oedipus, believe him! 632
Respect the oath he has just sworn before the gods
and before me and these people.

CHORUS

I beg you, allow yourself to be swayed,
my Lord, by your thought and your will. 636

OEDIPUS

In what do you wish me to yield?

CHORUS

Respect this man who never has been foolish
and is now made mighty by his oath.

OEDIPUS

Are you asking for something definite? 640

CHORUS

Yes.

OEDIPUS

Then tell me what it is.

CHORUS

That you do not subject your friend, who stands under sacred
oath,
to accusation, stripping him of honor with groundless words. 644

OEDIPUS

Know well that when you ask for this, you are asking
for my death or for my exile from this land.

CHORUS

No! By Helios,* the first among all gods,
may I perish most wretchedly, abandoned
by the gods, abandoned by friends,
if I harbored such a thought.
But the ruin of the land, alas,
will eat at my heart,
if to Thebes' old strife is added yours.

OEDIPUS

So let him go then, even if I must perish
or be driven from this land, stripped of honor.
But it is your poignant words, not his, that move me
to compassion. Him I shall loathe, wherever he might be.

CREON

It is clear that you yield with spite, but you will be downcast
when your rage passes. As is just, natures such as yours
are most painful to bear to themselves.

OEDIPUS

Just go and let me be!

CREON

I shall go, misunderstood by you, but still the same man in their eyes.

[Exit CREON]

CHORUS

Our Lady, why do you delay
to lead Oedipus into the palace?

*The sun, also a deity.

JOCASTA

I first want to know what has befallen here.

CHORUS

Opinions not based on evidence arose.
But even something mistaken can corrode.

JOCASTA

Was it just between the two of them?

CHORUS

Yes.

JOCASTA

And what was said?

CHORUS

I believe it is enough, enough!
Thinking of this land, this matter must end here.

OEDIPUS

Though you are of good judgment, do you see
what we have come to because you did not stand behind me,
because you calmed my passion?

CHORUS

My lord, I have said this more than once:
I would reveal myself as mad,
as incapable of sound thought,
should I turn my back on you, who,
when Thebes was reeling in despair,
restored it to its course.
Be once more our able captain!

JOCASTA

My lord, tell me, by the gods,
what it was that angered you so much.

OEDIPUS

I shall tell you, as I respect you more, my Lady,
than I do these others.

JOCASTA

Speak, and explain to me your angry accusations.

OEDIPUS

He says that I am the murderer of Laius.

JOCASTA

Does he say this from his own knowledge,
or did he learn it from someone else?

OEDIPUS

Creon involved that evildoing prophet,
to keep himself and his mouth unsoiled.

JOCASTA

Put aside this instant what you are saying.
Hear me, and learn that no mortal possesses
the art of prophecy, as I shall now prove to you.
Laius received an oracle—I will not say
from Apollo himself, but from one of his servants—
telling Laius that it was his fate to be killed by a son
born to him and me. And yet, as we are told,
he was murdered by foreign robbers where three roads cross.
Still, his son was not three days born when Laius
fastened his feet and had him cast by the hands of others
onto a remote mountainside. Hence Apollo
did not cause the child to become his father's murderer,
nor did Laius succumb to the calamity he feared,
falling victim to his son. And yet this was
the very thing the voices of the oracle had foretold.
So pay them no heed. When a god wants something
and seeks it, he will reveal it himself.

OEDIPUS
Hearing your words, my Lady,
my mind is shaken and my spirit reels.

JOCASTA
What fear and worry make you speak this way?

OEDIPUS
Did I hear you say that Laius
was slaughtered where three roads cross?

JOCASTA
That is what was and still is said.

OEDIPUS
Where did this incident happen?

JOCASTA
It was in the land called Phocis, where the roads meet
from Delphi and from Daulis.

OEDIPUS
How long ago did this take place?

JOCASTA
The city received the news
just before you were proclaimed our king.

OEDIPUS
O Zeus, what are your designs on me!

JOCASTA
What is it, Oedipus, that is weighing upon your heart?

OEDIPUS
Do not ask me yet. Tell me about Laius:
what did he look like, what was his age?

JOCASTA
His hair was dark, with the first sprinkles of white,

his appearance not unlike yours.

OEDIPUS

Alas! It seems I have unwittingly
exposed myself to a dreadful curse.

JOCASTA

What do you mean? My Lord, I shrink back when I look at you!

OEDIPUS

I am gripped by the dread that the prophet has the gift of sight.
You can shed light on this if you tell me one more thing.

JOCASTA

Though I am afraid, I shall listen, and will answer you.

OEDIPUS

Did Laius leave with a small group of soldiers,
or with a large one, as befits a king?

JOCASTA

There were five in all, one of them
a herald. Laius traveled in a chariot.

OEDIPUS

Ai ai! Now all is clear.
Who told you these things, my Lady?

JOCASTA

A slave who was the only one to escape.

OEDIPUS

Is he part of our household now?

JOCASTA

No. When he returned and saw that you were king,
with Laius dead, he begged me, clasping my hands,
to send him to distant pastures so that he

could be as far away from the city as possible.
I sent him there, for though he was a slave,
he deserved that and greater favors.

OEDIPUS

Can he come back here to us quickly?

JOCASTA

Yes, he can. But why do you ask this?

OEDIPUS

I fear, my Lady, that I might have said too much,
that is why I wish to see him.

JOCASTA

Then he shall come. But I believe I do deserve
to learn what is worrying you, my Lord.

OEDIPUS

I will not keep it from you, since I have reached
such a state of foreboding. To whom better can I speak
as I confront such a fate? Polybus of Corinth was my father,
my mother Merope, a Dorian. I was raised foremost among citizens
until fate brought about an incident that was to be wondered at,
but not of great import. At dinner there was a man
who had drunk too much, and over the wine
he called me a counterfeit son of my father. I was angered
and could barely control myself. But the next day
I went to my mother and father and questioned them.
They dealt harshly with the man who had spat out those words
and I was reassured, yet the words kept nagging at me,
circling in my mind. Without telling my mother and father
I went to Delphi, but Apollo sent me away, not deigning
to respond to my question but instead revealing to me, unhappy man,

terrible and wretched things: that I was fated to have intercourse
with my mother, that I would present mankind with a brood
it could not bear to look upon, and that I
would be the murderer of the father who begot me. 772
After hearing this, wandering by the stars, I left Corinth for a place
where I would never see the evil oracle's dreadful predictions fulfilled.
In my wanderings I came to where you say the king met his end.
And I shall tell you the truth, my Lady. As I walked 776
by where the three roads meet, I came upon a herald, and a man
just as you described, who was in a chariot drawn by horses.
The chariot driver and the man tried to push me out of the way,
and in anger I struck the driver who was forcing me off the road. 780
The older man waited for the moment when I passed his chariot,
and struck me in the middle of the head with his whip.
But he paid a greater penalty: swiftly I hit him with the staff
I held in this hand and he fell, tumbling backward out of the chariot. 784
I killed them all. If there is some connection
between that stranger and Laius, what man would be more wretched,
more hated by the gods than I? No foreigner or citizen
will be able to receive me in his house or speak a word to me, 788
but would have to turn me out. I alone, and no other man,
will have brought these curses down upon me. Polluting
the dead man's marriage bed with these hands that killed him.
Am I evil in nature? Am I not entirely impure? 792

Will I not have to leave in exile, in my banishment
never to see my loved ones nor ever again set foot
in my native land, where I would be compelled
to enter into wedlock with my mother and slay
my father Polybus, who begot and raised me?
Would one not be right to judge that this fate
was unleashed upon me by a cruel deity?
O pure and reverent gods, may I never, never,
see that day, but may I disappear from among men
before I look upon the stain of such a disaster.

CHORUS

For us, my Lord, this is frightening. But until you hear
from the man who was present, have hope.[6]

OEDIPUS

In truth that is my only hope, to wait
for that man, the shepherd, to come.

JOCASTA

Once he is here, what will you want of him?

OEDIPUS

I will explain. If he should still maintain what you are saying,
then I will have escaped this disaster.

JOCASTA

What did I say that was so extraordinary?

OEDIPUS

You said that he stated Laius was killed by robbers.
If he still says that it was a number of men,
then I am not the slayer. One cannot be many.
But if he clearly speaks of one man traveling alone,
then the deed falls on me.

JOCASTA

You can be certain that he reported it so,

and he cannot retract it now. The whole city heard him,
not I alone. But even if he should depart in any way
from what he said before, he will not, my Lord, be able
to prove that the prophecy of the killing of Laius still stands.
Apollo clearly proclaimed that Laius would die by my son's hand.
But that unfortunate child could not have slain him,
for he had perished first. So when it comes to prophecy,
I would look for neither this meaning nor that.

OEDIPUS

You are right. But still send someone
to bring the slave. Do not fail to do so.

JOCASTA

I will quickly send for him. But let us go back inside.
I would never do anything not pleasing to you.

[OEDIPUS and JOCASTA enter the palace]

CHORUS

May Destiny be at my side
so that I may win praise for reverent purity
in word and deed, as prescribed by laws
from on high, born from the ether,
Olympus alone their father.
Man's mortal nature did not beget these laws,
nor will oblivion ever lull them to sleep.
Great is the god within them, who never ages.

Tyranny begets Hubris, and if sated to excess
with what is not right or good,
Hubris will climb to the topmost pinnacle,
only to confront a sheer abyss where feet are of no avail.
Yet I pray to the god that he does not put a stop
to the struggling rivalry that brought good to the city.
Never will I cease to have the god as my protector.

But whoever is haughty in word or deed, 844
ignoring justice, not revering
the shrines of the gods:
may evil fortune seize him for his ill-fated pride
if he does not acquire his gains justly, 848
does not avoid what is sacrilegious,
if he recklessly violates the inviolate.
Who would be able to fend off
from him arrows of rage? 852
If such evil deeds are to be honored,
then why dance in honor of the gods?

If these oracles do not prove true,
so that man can point to them as infallible, 856
never again will I go chastely
to the hallowed navel of the earth,
nor to the temple of Abac,*
nor that of Olympia. 860
But Zeus, O divine sovereign,
if you are rightly to be called ruler of all,
let this not escape you and your immortal power.
For the oracles about Laius are fading, 864
disregarded by all, and Apollo's honor is dimmed.
The power of the gods is dying.

[JOCASTA emerges from the palace]

JOCASTA

Lords of this land, I have decided to go to the temples
of the gods, bearing these garlands and incense. 868
Oedipus' mind is burning beyond all measure
with every kind of anguish, not judging
the new in the light of the old, like a rational man,

---

*Wealthy temple in Phocis.

but at the mercy of anyone who speaks to him of terror.
Lycean Apollo! As I cannot help Oedipus with my counsel,
I come to you as a suppliant, for you are so near and close.
I come with the prayer that you resolve our plight,
for now we are in as much terror
as those who see the captain of their ship washed overboard.

[Enter a MESSENGER from Corinth]

MESSENGER

Can I learn from you, strangers, where I might find
the palace of King Oedipus? Or better,
tell me where he is, if you know.

CHORUS

This is his home, stranger, and he is within.
This is his wife and the mother of his children.

MESSENGER

May she rejoice as his honored wife
and mother of his children!

JOCASTA

May you too be happy, stranger, as you deserve
for your kind words. But tell me
what you have come for, or what you wish to tell us.

MESSENGER

I bring good news, my Lady, for your house and for your husband.

JOCASTA

What news is this, and who sends you?

MESSENGER

I come from Corinth. My news will definitely please you
—though, I suppose, it might sadden you too.

JOCASTA
What is it? How can it hold such double power?

MESSENGER
Word has it that the men of Corinth
wish to proclaim Oedipus their king.

JOCASTA
How can that be? Does not venerable Polybus still hold power?

MESSENGER
No, for death holds him in his tomb.

JOCASTA
What are you saying? Is Oedipus' father dead?

MESSENGER
If I do not speak the truth, I deserve to die.

JOCASTA *[to an attendant]*
Girl, go at once and tell the master.
Where are you now, prophesies of the gods?
Oedipus avoided Polybus for so long
out of fear of killing him, and now he has died
at the hands of fate, not at the hands of Oedipus.

[OEDIPUS comes out of the palace]

OEDIPUS
Jocasta, dearest wife,
why do you summon me from the palace?

JOCASTA
Listen to this man, and then ask
what has happened to the gods' hallowed oracles.

OEDIPUS
Who is this man, and what does he wish to tell me?

JOCASTA
He is from Corinth. He reports that your father,

Polybus, is no more. He has died.

OEDIPUS

What are you saying, stranger? Tell me the news yourself.

MESSENGER

If I have to tell you straight out,
then know that he is dead.

OEDIPUS

Was it by conspiracy or through sickness?

MESSENGER

A small tilt brings an old man's body to rest.

OEDIPUS

So it seems the poor man died of an illness.

MESSENGER

That, together with the many years he lived.

OEDIPUS

Alas, alas, why then, my Lady, should we seek out
the prophetic hearth of Pythia, or the birds
shrieking on high, whose interpreters augured that I
was to kill my father? He lies dead, deep within the earth,
while I am here, not having touched my sword,
unless he died of longing for me.
If that was so, then I brought about his death.
In any case, Polybus now lies in Hades,
and took all the worthless oracles with him.

JOCASTA

Is that not exactly what I said?

OEDIPUS

You did, but my fear led me astray.

JOCASTA

Do not let any of that worry you.

OEDIPUS

But how can I not fear my mother's bed?

JOCASTA

Man is in Fate's power, so why should he fear 932
what is to come? It is better to live life
as best one can. Do not live in terror of a marriage
to your mother. In dreams, too, many men
have had intercourse with their mothers. 936
But he who pays no heed to such things
bears life most easily.

OEDIPUS

Everything you say would be fine if the woman who bore me
were not still alive. As she lives, I have no choice 940
but to be afraid, even though what you say is right.

JOCASTA

Either way, your father's funeral is a great ray of light.

OEDIPUS

It is indeed. But I am afraid of the woman who is still alive.

MESSENGER

Who is this woman you are afraid of? 944

OEDIPUS

Merope, old man, the wife of Polybus.

MESSENGER

What is it about her that frightens you?

OEDIPUS

A terrible oracle from the gods, stranger.

MESSENGER

Can this oracle be revealed? Or is it not lawful for another to
know? 948

OEDIPUS

I can tell you. Apollo proclaimed that I was fated
to have intercourse with my mother, and that with my own hands
I would shed my father's blood. That is why I have lived
far from Corinth for so long. I have been fortunate, 952
and yet it is most sweet to look into one's parents' eyes.

MESSENGER

And was this the fear that kept you away from Corinth?

OEDIPUS

I did not want to be my father's murderer, old man.

MESSENGER

Well, my Lord, have I, coming here in good will, 956
not released you from this fear?

OEDIPUS

And you shall receive a reward worthy of your service.

MESSENGER

Indeed, I came in the hope that I would receive some benefit
from your coming home to Corinth. 960

OEDIPUS

But I will never go to where my parents are.

MESSENGER

Young man, it is very clear that you do not know what you are doing—

OEDIPUS

What do you mean, old man? Explain yourself.

MESSENGER

If you are not returning home because of them. 964

OEDIPUS

It is because I fear that Apollo's oracle may prove true.

MESSENGER

Do you mean you might be polluted by your parents?

OEDIPUS

Yes, old man. That is what I live in fear of.

MESSENGER

Do you not know you have no reason to be afraid? 968

OEDIPUS

How can that be, if I was born the son of those parents?

MESSENGER

Because Polybus was no relation to you.

OEDIPUS

What did you say? Polybus did not father me?

MESSENGER

He was just as much your father as I am. 972

OEDIPUS

How can my father be as much my father as a man who is nothing to me?

MESSENGER

Because neither he nor I fathered you.

OEDIPUS

Then how is it that he called me his son?

MESSENGER

Because, I tell you, he received you as a gift from my hands. 976

OEDIPUS

And yet he loved me greatly, though he received me from another's hands?

MESSENGER

He had been childless before.

OEDIPUS

Did you buy me, or give me to him after you found me?

MESSENGER

I found you in the craggy forests of Mount Cithaeron. 980

OEDIPUS

Why were you wandering there?

MESSENGER

I was charged with watching over a flock on the mountain.

OEDIPUS

You mean you were just a shepherd, a mere wanderer for hire?

MESSENGER

Yes my son, but I did prove your savior. 984

OEDIPUS

How was I when you took me in your arms?

MESSENGER

The ankles of your feet can bear witness.

OEDIPUS

Alas, what ancient evils are you voicing?

MESSENGER

Your ankles had been pierced, and I untied you. 988

OEDIPUS

A dreadful shame that I carried with me from my cradle.

MESSENGER

And it was from this fate that you received your name.*

OEDIPUS

By the gods! Tell me, was it my mother or my father who did this?

---

*Oedipus means "swollen foot" in Greek.

MESSENGER
I do not know, but he who gave you to me would.

OEDIPUS
So you did not find me, but I was given to you by another?

MESSENGER
No, I did not find you. Another shepherd gave you to me.

OEDIPUS
Who was he? Can you say?

MESSENGER
I think he was said to be one of Laius' men.

OEDIPUS
The man who once was king of this land?

MESSENGER
Yes. He was a shepherd of that king.

OEDIPUS
Is he still alive so that I can see him?

MESSENGER
You, the people of this land, would know that best.

OEDIPUS
Does anyone here present know the shepherd
of whom he speaks? Has anyone seen him
in the pastures, or here in the city?
Tell me, for the time has come to find things out.

CHORUS
I believe it is no other than the man from the pastures
whom you have already commanded to see.
But Jocasta could best tell you that.

OEDIPUS
My lady, do you know if the man we have just sent for

is the one of whom the stranger speaks?

JOCASTA

What does it matter of whom he speaks? Pay no heed.
Those pointless, foolish words deserve to be forgotten.

OEDIPUS

It cannot be that I would get such evidence
and not shed light on my birth.

JOCASTA

By the gods, if you care for your life, do not let your thoughts
linger on this. My own anguish is enough.

OEDIPUS

Take heart. Even if I prove thrice a slave,
you will not be shown as lowly.

JOCASTA

Heed my counsel, I beg you. Do not do this!

OEDIPUS

You cannot persuade me not to seek out the truth.

JOCASTA

And yet it is my good judgment that tells you what is best for you.

OEDIPUS

That "best" is what has tormented me so long.

JOCASTA

Unfortunate man, may you never find out who you are.[7]

OEDIPUS

Will someone bring me the shepherd?
And let this woman rejoice in her exalted family.

JOCASTA

Woe, woe, unhappy man!

That is all I can call you evermore.

[Exit JOCASTA]

CHORUS

Oedipus, why did the queen rush away
in such wild sorrow? I fear that evil
may burst forth from this silence.

OEDIPUS

Let what may burst forth! Even if I am
of humble birth, I want to know my origin
—though she, proud as women are,
seems ashamed of my lowly birth.
I see myself as the child of the fortune
that brings good and will not suffer dishonor.
Fortune is my mother, and the months are my family
which has defined me, great or small.
Being of such provenance, I would never be the kind of man
who would not want to learn his birth.

CHORUS

If I am a prophet
and skillful in my judgment,
then, by Olympus,
you, Mount Cithaeron,
tomorrow's full moon
shall exalt you
as Oedipus' compatriot,
nurse, and mother—
and we shall honor you with dances
for your kindness to our king.
O Apollo, to whom we call out,
may this be pleasing to you.

Which of the long-living nymphs,
my son, lay with mountain-roaming Pan

to sire you? Or was it
a bride of Apollo,
for the mountain pastures are dear to him?
Or did Cyllene's lord*
or the Bacchic god who dwells
on mountain tops receive you
from one of the dark-eyed nymphs
with whom he often frolics.

[Enter SHEPHERD]

OEDIPUS

If I too am to make conjectures, elders of Thebes,
then this man, though I have never met him, must be
the shepherd for whom we have long been searching.
His advanced years would match that man's, and furthermore
I recognize those who are accompanying him as my servants.
But in this case you surpass me in knowledge,
since you have seen the shepherd before.

CHORUS

Indeed, I recognize him. He was Laius' most trusted servant,
though only a shepherd.

OEDIPUS

First of all I ask you, Corinthian stranger,
is this the man you meant?

MESSENGER

Yes, this man you see before you.

OEDIPUS

You there, old man! Look at me and answer
whatever I ask you. Did Laius once own you?

---

*Cyllene is a mountain in Arcadia; its ruler is Hermes, a messenger god who links earth with the divine realms.

SHEPHERD

I was his slave—but raised in his home, not bought.

OEDIPUS

What was your work, how did you live?

SHEPHERD

For most of my life I have watched over flocks of sheep.

OEDIPUS

And in what regions?

SHEPHERD

There was Mount Cithaeron, but also the regions around it.

OEDIPUS

Then do you know this man? Did you meet him there?

SHEPHERD

Doing what? What man do you mean?

OEDIPUS

This man. Have you ever had dealings with him?

SHEPHERD

I cannot say that I remember him offhand.

MESSENGER

It is no wonder, my Lord. But though
he does not recognize me,
I shall help him remember clearly.
For I am certain he will recall
that we were together three times by Mount Cithaeron,
each time for half a year, from spring
to the rising of the star Arcturus.
He with two flocks, I with one. Come winter,
I would drive my sheep back to their pens,
and he his to those of Laius. Was it as I say, or was it not?

SHEPHERD
You speak the truth, but all that was long ago.

MESSENGER
So tell me then, do you recall giving me
a child to bring up as my own?

SHEPHERD
What is this? Why are you asking me these questions?

MESSENGER
Here is the man, my friend, who was that child.

SHEPHERD
Go to your ruin! Be silent!

OEDIPUS
Old man! Do not rebuke him!
It is your words that deserve rebuke.

SHEPHERD
Noblest of masters, how did I offend?

OEDIPUS
By not speaking of the child he asks about.

SHEPHERD
That is because he wastes his efforts, speaking of things of which he knows nothing.

OEDIPUS
If you will not speak at my pleasure, then you will do so from pain.

SHEPHERD
No, by the gods! You would not torture an old man!

OEDIPUS
Tie his hands behind his back!

SHEPHERD
O ill-fated man! What do you wish to know?

OEDIPUS

Did you give him the child he is asking about?

SHEPHERD

I did. I wish I had died that very day!

OEDIPUS

Die you will, if you do not tell me the truth.

SHEPHERD

My destruction is even more certain if I do.

OEDIPUS

This man, it seems, is trying to drag out the matter.

SHEPHERD

No—indeed I have already said that I gave him the child.

OEDIPUS

Where did you get it? Was it your own, or someone else's?

SHEPHERD

It was not my own. I was given it by another.

OEDIPUS

From which of these citizens, from what house?

SHEPHERD

No, master! Do not ask me further, by the gods!

OEDIPUS

You are dead if I must ask you once more.

SHEPHERD

Well then, the child was from the house of Laius.

OEDIPUS

A slave, or of his family?

SHEPHERD

Woe, I am about to speak the terrible truth.

OEDIPUS

And I am about to hear it. But it must be heard.

SHEPHERD

It was said to be his child. But your wife,
inside the palace, she can best explain.

OEDIPUS

Was she the one who gave it to you?

SHEPHERD

Yes, my Lord.

OEDIPUS

For what purpose?

SHEPHERD

To kill it.

OEDIPUS

The poor woman, had she borne it?

SHEPHERD

It was in fear of the evil prophecies.

OEDIPUS

What prophecies?

SHEPHERD

It was said that the child would kill its parents.

OEDIPUS

Then why did you leave it with this old man?

SHEPHERD

I felt pity, master, and thought he would take it to another land,
the land from which he came. But he saved the child
for the greatest evils, because if you are who he says you are,
then know that you were born to a wretched fate.

OEDIPUS

Woe, woe! All has proven true! O light,
I now look on you for the last time! All has been revealed!
I was born from whom I should not have been born,
I have consorted with whom I should not have consorted,
killed whom I should not have killed.

CHORUS

Woe, generations of man,
O how I count your life
as nothingness. What man,
gains more happiness, what man,
than just enough to make him believe
he is happy before he falls into decline.
With your fate as example,
your fate decreed by the god, unhappy Oedipus,
nothing in the life of man is to be deemed happy.

You shot your arrow beyond its limit,
winning success not always
smiled upon by the gods
after you destroyed the taloned maiden,
the prophecying Sphinx,
and stood firm for my city
like a tower against death.
That is why we honored you so greatly
and summoned you as our king
to rule mighty Thebes.

But now who can be called
more miserable than you?
Who lives in more torment,
in more cruel pain
through reversal in life?
Woe, glorious Oedipus,
the same great harbor

you entered as bridegroom
served as marriage bed for son and father.
How, oh how, wretched man,
could the furrows that your father ploughed
endure you for so long in silence?

Time that sees all
has exposed you against your will,
and long ago condemned your marriage
that was no marriage, in which you
were both begotten and begetter.
Woe, son of Laius, I wish, how I wish,
I had never set eyes on you!
How I grieve,
lamentation pours from my mouth.
But to speak the truth,
from you I drew a breath of life,
you soothed my tired eyes in sleep.

[Enter SECOND MESSENGER from the palace]

SECOND MESSENGER

Most honored elders of this land!
What deeds will you now hear and see,
what mourning will you bear,
if you are beholden to the house of Laius.
For I believe that all the waters of Ister or Phasis*
cannot wash clean this house, so many are the horrors,
intended and unintended, that it hides,
some of which shall now come to light,
for self-inflicted torments bring the most pain.

CHORUS

What we already know is worthy of grieving

---

*Ister: the river Danube. Phasis: remote river beyond the Black Sea.

and lamentation. What can you add to this?

SECOND MESSENGER

There is most urgent news to proclaim
and hear: our most august Jocasta is dead!

CHORUS

O most miserable of women! What was the cause?

SECOND MESSENGER

It was her own deed. You have been spared
the most distressing part, for you did not see it.
But from what I can report you will learn
the torments of that wretched woman.
Frantic in her grief, she rushed through the gates
toward her bridal bed. She tore at her hair with both hands,
slamming shut the doors behind her, calling out to Laius,
now long dead, reminding him of the seed he had sown
so long ago, a seed that had brought him death,
telling Laius that he had left her to bear
accursed offspring by his son. She wept over the bed
where in double progeny she had borne a husband
from her husband, and children from her child.
How she then killed herself I do not know,
for Oedipus burst into the palace screaming,
so we did not witness her woe to its end.
We saw him tearing through the halls,
begging for a sword, asking for his wife
who was not his wife but a maternal field
that had doubly sprouted him and his children.
As he raged, some god revealed her to him,
it was none of us men who were standing nearby.
As if led there, he threw himself with a terrible cry
against the double doors, which cracked
and broke inward in their frame, and hurled himself
into the room. There we all saw the woman hanging,

tangled in a knotted cord. He sees her, the unhappy man,
shouts out, and tears down the noose. The wretched woman
lay on the ground, and what happened next
was most terrible to behold. He tore off the golden pins
that fastened her dress, raised them high,[8] and plunged them
into the sockets of his eyes, crying out that now his eyes
would see neither his suffering nor his evil deeds—
from now on his eyes would see in darkness
what he should never have seen, they would not recognize
those he wanted to recognize. Chanting these words,
he kept plunging the pins, not once, but many times,
raising his eyes up toward them. The bleeding sockets
soaked his cheeks, not with oozing drops,
but a dark spray of bloody showering hail. These evils
did not descend upon the head of one alone, but on two,
the entwined evils of man and woman.
Their earlier happiness may have been true,
but now, this day, there is lament and ruin,
death and disgrace. No evil that has a name is absent.

CHORUS

And does the poor wretch have any respite now from pain?

SECOND MESSENGER

He is shouting for someone to open the gates
so all Thebes can behold the man who is his father's killer,
his mother's—I cannot utter the sacrilegious words he
spoke! —,
shouting to have himself banished from the city, and not
linger
in the house under the curse he had brought upon himself.
But he is lacking strength and needs a guide,
for his affliction is too great to bear. But you
shall see all this yourself. The doors of the portal
are opening, and you will behold a sight
to lead even one who hates him to pity.

[Enter OEDIPUS]

CHORUS

O torment terrible for man to behold, torment
worse than I have ever encountered!
What madness seized you, O wretched man?
What god leapt further in your ungodly destiny
than the furthest leaps? Woe, woe, unhappy man,
I cannot bear to look at you, though I want to ask so many
questions,
hear so many answers, peer into so many things;
Such is the shuddering horror you arouse in me.

OEDIPUS

Ai, Ai! Wretch that I am!
Where am I being carried in my misery?
Where will my voice fly on the wings of the air?
Alas, O god, how far you leaped!

CHORUS

He has leaped to a dreadful extreme, never before heard or seen.

OEDIPUS

Woe! My cloud of darkness,
from which one can only turn away in horror,
its inexpressible onslaught sped by an ill wind.
Alas!
I say again, alas! How the spikes of those pins
and the memory of evil bore into me.

CHORUS

It is no wonder that with these torments
you should doubly mourn a double evil.

OEDIPUS

Ah, my friend,
you have stayed here as my steadfast companion,
have remained to take care of this blind man.

Woe, woe!
I know it is you who has remained,
for even in my darkness I recognize your voice.

CHORUS

What a dreadful deed you have done! How could you
venture to quench your sight? Which of the gods drove you to this?

OEDIPUS

It was Apollo, Apollo, my friends,
who wrought these most evil of evil sufferings.
But it was my own hand and no other that struck my eyes,
wretch that I am, for of what use is it for me to see
when nothing I can look upon is sweet?

CHORUS

It is as you say.

OEDIPUS

What is there for me to see or cherish,
what word to hear with joy, my friends?
Take me from this place as quickly as you can,
take me away, my friends, most worthless man that I am,
most accursed, most hated of mortals by the gods.

CHORUS

Wretched is your mind and wretched your fate!
How I wish that you had never known.

OEDIPUS

A curse on him who freed me from my cruel fetters,
rescued me, and saved me from death.
He did me no favor!
Had I died
I would not have caused such distress to those I love.

CHORUS

I too would wish it had been so.

OEDIPUS

I would not have become my father's killer,
nor would men have called me bridegroom
of the woman who bore me.
Now I am abandoned by the gods, the son
of profane parents who shared his father's marriage bed.
If there is evil greater than evil, that lot has fallen
to Oedipus.

CHORUS

It would have been better for you to be no more, than to
live in blindness:
I do not know how that decision can be considered wise.

OEDIPUS

Do not tell me that things were not done best.
Give me no more advice. I do not know with what eyes
I could look upon my father when I descend to Hades,
nor upon my wretched mother. Against both
I have committed acts for which hanging would not suffice.
Or could I wish to gaze upon my children, born
as they were born? No, not with my eyes. Nor upon the city,
or the towers, or the sacred statues of the gods.
I, most wretched, have deprived myself of all this, I
who was once raised to be foremost among Thebans,
proclaiming that all should cast out the impious one
revealed by the gods as impure and the son of Laius.
After proclaiming this infamy as mine,
was I to look these citizens in the eye? Never!
Could I have blocked the stream of sound from my ears,
so that I would be deaf as well as blind,
I would have shut away my miserable body entirely.
It is sweet for the mind to live apart from misery.

Alas, Mount Cithaeron! Why did you receive me?
Why did you not kill me right away,
so that I would not reveal to mankind of whom I was born?
O Polybus! And Corinth, you, the ancient place of my ancestors
only in name! With what beauty you raised me
beneath which evil festered! For now
I am revealed to be evil and of evil ancestry.
O three roads and hidden gully! O thicket and narrow pass
where the three roads meet! You drank my father's blood,
my blood, shed by my own hand! Do you still remember
the deeds you witnessed there, and the deeds I did here?
O marriage, marriage! You gave birth to me and then
sprouted seed from the same seed, bringing forth
brothers, fathers, sons of incestuous blood,
brides who were wives and mothers, most shameful human deeds.
But as it is ugly to do such deeds and also to speak of them,
you must, by the gods, hide me as soon as possible
away from Thebes to where you will never set eyes on me again,
or kill me, or throw me into the sea. Come!
Do not shrink back from touching a wretch!
Hear my words, fear not!
My evils can be borne by no other mortal but myself.

[Enter CREON]

CHORUS

Just as you ask this, Creon arrives opportunely
to act and to decide, for he remains
the sole custodian of this land in your place.

CREON

I have not come to mock you, Oedipus,
nor avenge prior wrongs.

[To the bystanders]

If you feel no shame before mankind, at least
feel shame before divine Helios and the flames
of his sun that feed the world. Do not cast away
uncovered this polluted man, whom neither earth
nor sacred rain nor light will welcome.
Lead him immediately into the house, for piety demands
that family alone can see and hear the evils of their kin.

OEDIPUS

Beyond my expectations you, the best of men, have come to me,
the most evil, and so I ask you by the gods to grant me a favor,
one that is in your interest, and not mine.

CREON

What is the favor that you ask of me?

OEDIPUS

Banish me from this land as quickly as you can
to where no mortal can address me.

CREON

I would do so, I assure you, but first
I want to learn from Apollo how to proceed.

OEDIPUS

But his oracle was clear: that I, the profane,
the killer of his father, must be destroyed.

CREON

That was the oracle, but as we have come to such a dire circumstance,
we must find out exactly what to do.

OEDIPUS

You would approach the oracle on behalf of a wretched

man like me?

CREON

Yes, for surely now even you would believe the god. 1380

OEDIPUS

And yet it is to you I turn, on you I rely to arrange
whatever burial you would like for her who is inside the house.
It is right that you be the one to decide this for one of your own.
As for me, let it not be thought fitting for me to live in this city of my fathers. 1384
Let me dwell in the mountains, on my own Mount Cithaeron, which,
when they were still alive, my mother and my father had chosen for my tomb.
That way my death will come from those who had sought to kill me.
I know well that no sickness or other ill can destroy me: 1388
I would not have been saved from death except for some terrible evil.
But let my fate take its course. As for my children, Creon,
you need not trouble yourself about the boys.
They are men and will find their way wherever they go. 1392
But take care of my two pitiful and wretched girls, whose table
was never set apart from mine so that they would never be without me,
and who always shared whatever food I ate. Let me touch them and lament.
I beseech you, my Lord, you of noble birth. Come, if I can touch them, 1396
I shall feel as if they were with me as when I could see.
But wait! By the gods, do I not hear my beloved girls weeping?
Creon in his compassion has sent me my dearest ones,

my offspring—am I right?

CREON

You are. I arranged it, foreseeing your joy.

OEDIPUS

May you prosper, and may some god protect you better
than I was protected. My children, where are you?
Come to your brother's hands that performed their duty to the eyes,
once shining, of the father who begot you! The father
who unseeing, unknowing, became, O children, your father
where he himself was conceived. I shed tears for you.
I cannot see you, but I think of the misery of the rest of your lives
among men. To what gathering of citizens will you go,
from what feasts will you not return home in tears
instead of rejoicing in the spectacle? And when
you reach the age of marriage, who, my children, who would risk
receiving the disastrous censure that would have been leveled
against your parents? What evil is lacking? Your father killed his father.
He ploughed his mother in the place where he was sown,
and so acquired you from where he himself was born.
Reproached with this, who will marry you? No one, my children.
Unmarried, you will wither in barrenness.
Son of Menoeceus, as you are the only father left to these two girls,
since the two of us who gave birth to them have perished,
do not look on as they wander beggars and husbandless.
They are your kin—do not diminish them to the level of evils that are mine.
Seeing them bereft at such a young age of everything
except for what you might give, have pity on them.

Agree to this and touch me with your hand.
To you, my children, were you old enough to understand,
I would give much advice. But as things are, I ask you
to pray that you may live where chance will allow,
and that you will have a better life than that of your father who begat you.

CREON
You have shed enough tears. Now go inside the house.

OEDIPUS
I must obey, though I do not go with pleasure.

CREON
Everything is good in its season.

OEDIPUS
Do you know on what condition I will go inside?

CREON
You will tell me, and having heard I shall know.

OEDIPUS
That you will send me away from this land.

CREON
What you ask of me is for Apollo to give.

OEDIPUS
But I have come to be most hated by the gods.

CREON
In that case you will soon have your wish.

OEDIPUS
Do you mean it?

CREON
It is not my way to say in vain things that I do not think.

OEDIPUS

Then you can take me away now.

CREON

Go, but leave your children here.

OEDIPUS

No! Do not take them from me!

CREON

Do not seek to keep everything in your power. The power
that was once yours did not accompany you for all your days.

CHORUS

Dwellers of our native city of Thebes, behold!
This is Oedipus,
who solved the infamous riddle
and was the most mighty of men,
on whose fortune no citizen could look without envy,
but who was overtaken by a wave of dreadful disaster!
Hence one should always look to man's final day,
and call no mortal happy until he has crossed
the end of life without suffering grief.

OEDIPUS AT COLONUS

CHARACTERS

OEDIPUS	former king of Thebes
ANTIGONE	daughter of Oedipus and Jocasta
ISMENE	Antigone's sister
A STRANGER	inhabitant of Colonus
CHORUS	of elders of Colonus
THESEUS	king of Athens
CREON	present king of Thebes and brother of Jocasta
POLYNICES	first son of Oedipus
A MESSENGER	

Non-speaking

Guards and attendants of Theseus

Bodyguards of Creon

Servant to Ismene

[In the sacred grove of the Eumenides (also known as Erinyes or Furies), outside Colonus, not far from Athens. Near the grove is a statue of Colonus, a legendary horseman. OEDIPUS and ANTIGONE enter the grove.]

OEDIPUS

Antigone, daughter of a blind old man, what land
have we come to? Who are the men of this city?
Who will welcome wandering Oedipus today
with meager gifts? I ask for little and am given even less,
though that is enough for me. Time and suffering,
ever my companions, and my noble blood
have taught me to endure. But, my child, if you see
any place I can sit down, either on profane ground
or in a grove sacred to the gods, stop and let me rest,
so that we can find out where we are. As strangers,
we must listen to the citizens, and do as they tell us.

ANTIGONE

Oedipus, my poor father, I see towers in the distance,
enclosing a city. And I believe this place is sacred,
as I see a lush growth of laurels, olive trees, and vines.
Richly-feathered nightingales are singing sweetly within.
Sit down on this unhewn rock,
for you have walked a long way for an old man.

OEDIPUS

Let me sit here, but remember to watch over me in my blindness.

ANTIGONE

You need not remind me, after all this time.

OEDIPUS

Do you know where we are?

ANTIGONE

I know that we are near Athens, but I do not know exactly where.

OEDIPUS

Indeed, the travelers along the road have told us.

ANTIGONE

Shall I go ask what place this is?

OEDIPUS

Yes, my child, find out if this place is inhabited.

ANTIGONE

It certainly is. But it seems I do not need to go,
for I see a man approaching.

OEDIPUS

Is he coming toward us?

[Enter STRANGER]

ANTIGONE

He is already here. Say what is fitting,
as the man now stands before you.

OEDIPUS

Stranger, I hear from this maiden, who sees for me
as well as for herself, that you have come at an opportune moment
to inform us of what we do not know.

STRANGER

Before you ask me anything, come out from the sanctuary,
for it is sacrilege to step on that hallowed ground.

OEDIPUS

What place is this? What god's sanctuary?

STRANGER

It must not be touched, no one may remain within it.
It belongs to the terrible goddesses,
the daughters of Earth and Darkness.*

*The Furies, deities of vegeance who pursue wrongdoers.

OEDIPUS

What is their venerable name, so I may invoke them in prayer?

STRANGER

The people here call them the all-seeing Eumenides,
the Kindly Ones. But elsewhere other names are favored.

OEDIPUS

May they receive their suppliant graciously,
for I will never leave this sanctuary.

STRANGER

What do you mean?

OEDIPUS

It is the sign of my fate.

STRANGER

I would not take it upon myself to force you to leave
without first reporting to the city and receiving orders.

OEDIPUS

By the gods, stranger, do not refuse what I beg you
to tell me, poor wanderer that I am.

STRANGER

What is it you want to know? I shall not refuse you an answer.

OEDIPUS

What is this place we have come to?

STRANGER

Listen and I shall tell you all I know. This whole area
is sacred. It belongs to holy Poseidon, but the Titan
Prometheus, the divine bearer of fire, resides here too.
The ground on which you stand is called the Bronze Threshold[1]
of this land, the rampart of Athens. The land all around
claims Colonus, the great horseman, as its founder,

and bears his name, as do all the people here.
This place is not honored in legend, stranger,
but honored by those who live here.

OEDIPUS

So there are people who live here?

STRANGER

Yes, there are. They take their name from the divine Colonus.

OEDIPUS

Does someone rule them, or does the word rest with the people?

STRANGER

The King of Athens rules them.

OEDIPUS

And who is he that rules in word and deed?

STRANGER

He is called Theseus, the son of Aegeus, our former king.

OEDIPUS

Can you send someone to go to him?

STRANGER

For what purpose? To bring him a message, or bid him to come?

OEDIPUS

For the purpose of affording me a little help,
from which he will reap great gains.

STRANGER

What great gains can he expect from one who cannot see?

OEDIPUS

There will be vision in the words I shall speak to him.

STRANGER

I discern from your countenance, stranger, that you are noble
despite your ill fortune. Stay here in the place where I found you
so you will not come to any harm, and I shall speak to the men
of Colonus, not those of Athens. These men will decide
whether you can remain or must go on your way.

[Exit STRANGER]

OEDIPUS

Has the stranger left us, my child?

ANTIGONE

He has gone, Father, you can speak freely
without worry, as I alone am here.

OEDIPUS

O fierce-eyed goddesses! As the first sanctuary in this land
at which I rest is yours, be not unfavorable to Apollo or to me.
Apollo prophesied many evils for me, but revealed
that after long years I would find rest in a land
where the deities would offer me refuge and hospitality.
Here I could come to the end of my wretched life,
a benefit for those who receive me and take me in,
but ruin for those who chased me and drove me out.
There were to be signs: an earthquake, great thunder,
a bolt of lightning from Zeus. I now understand
that it was a clear omen that led me along the road
to this grove, otherwise I, a sober wanderer, would never
in all my journeys have encountered you first, abstemious goddesses,[2]
nor would I have sat on this unhewn rock. O goddesses,
if I do not seem to you too insignificant, a perpetual slave
to the greatest hardships of mankind, grant a conclusion,
an ending to my life, as Apollo's oracles foretold. Come,
sweet daughters of ancient Darkness, and you, Athens,

most worthy of cities, named after supreme Pallas Athena,
take pity on the miserable shadow of Oedipus, for I am not the man I was.

ANTIGONE

Be silent, Father, some elders are approaching to see where you are sitting.

OEDIPUS

I will be silent, but lead me away from the road
and hide me in the grove until I have heard
what they are going to say.

CHORUS

Look for him. Who can he be?
Where is he? Where did he go,
this most impudent, most impudent
of men? Look for him, find him,
search everywhere! A wanderer,
the old man is a wanderer, he is not
from this land, or he would not
have entered the untrodden grove
of the invincible maidens
we tremble to name,
whom we pass with eyes averted,
without sound, without word,
our lips moving in silent propitious thought.
But now we hear that a man has come
who does not stand in dread of them,
though as I look around the sacred precinct,
I cannot see where he might be.

OEDIPUS

Here! I am that man. I see
with my voice, one could say.

CHORUS

Woe, woe,
he is terrible to behold, terrible to hear.

OEDIPUS

I beg you, do not look on me as lawless.

CHORUS

Zeus, our protector, who can this old man be?

OEDIPUS

Not, guardians of this land, a man to be envied for having had
the best of fortunes! That must be clear enough, otherwise
I would not be making my way with the eyes of another,
or be leaning, big as I am, on one so small.

CHORUS

Ah, have your eyes been blind
since you were born? Your life,
it seems, has been sad and long.
But I will strive to keep you
from adding this curse to your sorrows.
Stop, you are stepping too far, too far!
You must not tread that grove of silence
where a bowl of water is mixed with libations
of liquid honey. Take care, hapless stranger!
Turn around! Come back! You have gone too far!
Can you even hear me, long-suffering wanderer?
If you have anything to tell me,
come away from the untrodden ground
and speak where it is lawful
for all to speak. But until then, refrain!

OEDIPUS

My daughter, which way should we decide?

ANTIGONE

Father, we must do as these citizens urge,

we must yield and listen.

OEDIPUS

Then take hold of my hand.

ANTIGONE

Here it is.

OEDIPUS

Strangers, let me not suffer injustice 152
if I trust you and come out of here.

CHORUS

No one, venerable old man, shall ever
remove you from this place against your will.

OEDIPUS

Shall I walk still farther? 156

CHORUS

Yes, a little farther.

OEDIPUS

Farther?

CHORUS

Lead him, maiden, for you can see.

ANTIGONE

Follow me, follow me with your unseeing feet 160
to where I take you.

[Lines missing in the Greek text]

CHORUS

Unhappy man, stranger in a strange land,
resolve to loathe whatever this city regards as hateful,
and venerate what it esteems. 164

OEDIPUS

Guide me then, my daughter,

to ground where piety
will allow us to speak and listen
without battling necessity.

CHORUS

Stop. Do not move your foot beyond that ledge of natural rock.

OEDIPUS

Like this?

CHORUS

Enough, as I told you.

OEDIPUS

Shall I sit?

CHORUS

Yes, if you turn and crouch down, you can sit on the edge of that rock.

ANTIGONE

Father, I shall help you. Put one foot carefully after the other—

OEDIPUS

Alas, alas!

ANTIGONE

—leaning your aged body on my loving arm.

OEDIPUS

Alas for my sorrowful state.

CHORUS

Poor, long-suffering man,
now that you are settled,
tell us of whom you were born.
Who are you, led along in such pain?
Which is your native land?

OEDIPUS

Strangers, I am a banished man. But you must not—

CHORUS

What is it you forbid us, old man?

OEDIPUS

—do not, oh do not ask me
who I am, nor probe any further.

CHORUS

Why not?

OEDIPUS

My birth was terrible.

CHORUS

Speak.

OEDIPUS

My daughter, alas, what can I say?

CHORUS

Speak, stranger, what is the line
of your birth from your father's side?

OEDIPUS

Alas, what is to become of me, my child?

ANTIGONE

Speak, as your end is near.

OEDIPUS

Then I shall speak, as I cannot hide the truth.

CHORUS

You are delaying too long. Speak!

OEDIPUS

Do you know of Laius' son?

CHORUS
Oh, woe, woe!

OEDIPUS
And of the house of Labdacus?

CHORUS
O Zeus!

OEDIPUS
And of wretched Oedipus?

CHORUS
Can it be that you are he?

OEDIPUS
Do not be alarmed by what I say.

CHORUS
Alas, woe, woe!

OEDIPUS
I am ill-fated!

CHORUS
Woe, woe!

OEDIPUS
My daughter, what will happen to me?

CHORUS
Out! Leave our land now!

OEDIPUS
But what about your promises to me?

CHORUS
No doom will descend upon one who repays
what he has first been made to suffer.[3]
One deceit leading to other deceits will bring pain,
not delight. Leave this sanctuary now,

go from our land, so that you do not bring
a great burden upon our city.

ANTIGONE

Compassionate strangers!
At least have pity on me if you cannot bear
to listen to my aged father, now that you know
the acts he once unwittingly committed.
Miserable as I am, I beseech you, strangers,
on his behalf. I look into your eyes with eyes
that are not blind, as if I were of your own blood,
begging you to accord respect to this poor man.
We wretched ones are in your hands, as if you were gods.
I beg you by whatever you love: a child, a woman,
a cherished object, a god! You can never find a mortal
able to escape from where a god is leading him.

CHORUS

We assure you, daughter of Oedipus,
that we do pity you and your father
for your misfortune. But we tremble
at what the gods might send us,
and cannot bring ourselves to say more
than what we said to you just now.

OEDIPUS

What is the benefit of the splendor and glory
of Athens, if you let them flow away in vain?
They say that Athens is a paragon of piety,
that it alone can protect a distressed stranger,
that it alone can save him. What help is that to me
when you have made me rise from my supplication
in this sanctuary only to chase me away from fear of my name.
It is not me that you fear, nor my deeds.
If you compel me to speak of my mother and father,

which is what makes you fearful, then I suffered those deeds
more than I committed them. I know this well.
How can I be evil by nature when I only struck back
at what was done to me? Even had I acted consciously,
it would not have made me evil. I acted entirely unaware,
while those who made me suffer destroyed me in all awareness.
Therefore, strangers, I beseech you by the gods:
just as you made me leave this sanctuary, now protect me.
Do not profess to honor the gods and then turn your backs on them.
You can be certain that their eyes are upon those among mortals
who are pious, but also upon the impious, and no profane man
has ever escaped them. Do not shroud the hallowed prosperity
of Athens in their name by yielding to sacrilegious deeds,
but as you received me under pledge as a suppliant, preserve
and protect me. Do not dishonor me now that you have beheld
my hideous face, for I come in sacred reverence, bringing benefit
to the people of this city. When the king who rules you arrives,
you shall hear and know all—but until then, do not act as evil men.

CHORUS

I am compelled to regard your arguments with awe,
old man, for your words have not been spoken lightly.
It is enough for me that the rulers of this land will decide what to do.

OEDIPUS

Where is the king of this land, strangers?

CHORUS

He is in his father's city. The same man who saw you first
and called me here has gone to summon him.

OEDIPUS

Do you think he will have so much regard or concern
for a blind man that he would come here in person?

CHORUS

He surely will when he hears your name.

OEDIPUS

But who would have informed the king of my name?

CHORUS

It is a long road, but the travelers' tales are bound to reach him.
When he hears them he will certainly come.
Your name, old man, is so well-known
that even were he weighed down with sleep, he would hurry.

OEDIPUS

May he then come with good fortune for the city
and for me. What able man does not know his own good?

ANTIGONE

O Zeus! What can I say, what am I to think, Father?

OEDIPUS

What is it, Antigone my child?

ANTIGONE

I see a woman
riding toward us on a fine steed—she is wearing
a Thessalian hat to shade her face from the sun!
I am not sure? Is it her? Is it not? Is my mind deceiving me?
First I am certain, then not, and in my misery
I am at a loss for words! But it can be no one else!
Her radiant eyes are greeting me as she approaches,
signifying that most certainly it is . . . my beloved Ismene.

OEDIPUS

What are you saying, my child?

ANTIGONE

That I see your daughter, my very own sister.
Now you will hear her voice and recognize her.

[Enter ISMENE]

ISMENE

Father and Sister, the two sweetest names to me!
How hard it was to find you, and how hard
it is now to see you through my sorrow.

OEDIPUS

My child, have you really come?

ISMENE

O Father, in what misfortune do I see you!

OEDIPUS

My child, are you here?

ISMENE

Yes, after so many ordeals.

OEDIPUS

Touch me, my child.

ISMENE

I embrace you both.

OEDIPUS

My children, blood of my blood.

ISMENE

O miserable life!

OEDIPUS

Do you mean your sister's and mine?

ISMENE

And my life as well.

OEDIPUS

My child, why did you come?

ISMENE

Out of worry for you.

OEDIPUS

Were you longing to see me?

ISMENE

To see you and bring you news,
accompanied by my single trusted servant.

OEDIPUS

But where are your brothers, what are they doing?

ISMENE

They are where they are. A most terrible strife has erupted
between them.

OEDIPUS

Oh how the natures and lives of those two call to mind
the customs of Egypt! There men sit at home weaving,
while their women venture out to provide a livelihood.
This is how it is with you, my daughters. The men
who should be shouldering the labor you now bear
remain at home tending the house like maidens,
while the two of you have taken on the hardships
of your unfortunate father. You, Antigone,
since you emerged robust from a nurtured childhood,
have always wandered with me in misery, an old man's guide,
often roaming hungry and barefoot through wild forests,
tortured by rain and scorching sun, a miserable girl,
placing the comforts of home second to the needs of her father.
And you, Ismene, have once before, in secret from the
Thebans,
come to your father to tell him of the further prophecies
that have been foretold, and you have been the faithful guardian

of my name after I was driven from the city.
What news do you bring your father now, Ismene?
What is it that made you leave the house?
You cannot have come for nothing.
I am certain you bring me cause for dread.

ISMENE

I shall not recount what I suffered in seeking you out, Father,
as I do not want to endure it twice, once in the suffering
and again in the retelling. I have come to let you know
of the plight of your two ill-fated sons. At first
they were content to leave the throne to Creon
and not pollute the city, as they looked clear-eyed
on the ancient curse of our blood, which had filled
your house with misery. But now a god and their perversity
have sparked the thrice-wretched quest of each to seize
the rule and royal power. The younger in age
has deprived first-born Polynices of the throne,
and driven him from the city. And Polynices,
I heard in Thebes, has fled to Argos and there
acquired a new allegiance through marriage
and staunch allies in war, so that the honor of Thebes
will either be vanquished or raised to the sky.
Father, these are not just empty words,
but the terrible truth. I still cannot see
when the gods will finally take pity on your plight!

OEDIPUS

Do you have hope that the gods will look kindly upon me,
that I might finally be saved?

ISMENE

Yes, I do, Father. New prophecies have given me hope.

OEDIPUS

What are these prophecies? What have the oracles foretold, my child?

ISMENE

That if the men of Thebes wish to prosper
they will have to seek you out, whether you are dead or alive.

OEDIPUS

Who can hope to reap benefit from a man like me?

ISMENE

The oracles say that you will become the source of Theban power.

OEDIPUS

So when I am a dead man I shall again be alive?

ISMENE

The gods will now raise you up once more; before, they were destroying you.

OEDIPUS

It is a paltry thing to raise up an old man who was cast down as a youth.

ISMENE

And yet, know that for this reason Creon himself
will come, and very soon.

OEDIPUS

To do what, my daughter? Explain all this to me.

ISMENE

To place your tomb near Theban soil, where they can keep you
in their power without your crossing the boundaries of the city.

OEDIPUS

But what benefit can they reap from my remaining outside their gates?

ISMENE

It would weigh heavily on them if your grave were dishonored.

OEDIPUS

Even without a god's prophecy one could understand that.

ISMENE

That is why they want you near their land, so that they have power over you.

OEDIPUS

Will they cover me with Theban earth?

ISMENE

That, Father, the blood of your kindred will not permit. 372

OEDIPUS

Then they shall never have power over me.

ISMENE

That is bound to weigh heavily on the Thebans.

OEDIPUS

How will that come about, my child?

ISMENE

Through your anger, when they approach your tomb. 376

OEDIPUS

My child, where did you learn what you are telling me?

ISMENE

From men sent as envoys to the Delphic hearth.*

OEDIPUS

Did Apollo† truly proclaim that about me?

ISMENE

That is what the men who returned to the plains of Thebes reported. 380

---

*Delphi is the site of the most famous oracle in ancient Greece.

†God of prophecy.

OEDIPUS

Did either of my two sons hear this?

ISMENE

Both heard it, and know it well.

OEDIPUS

Those evil villains! Even though they heard it,
they put their kingship before their care for me?

ISMENE

I am pained at hearing these words, but I must bear the truth.

OEDIPUS

May the gods never quell their predestined strife,
and may the outcome of the battle on which they are bent
and for which they are now raising their spears depend on me.
May neither the one who now holds the scepter and throne prevail,
nor he who is banished ever return! For when I, who begot them,
was cast from my father's city in shame, they did not prevent it!
They did not defend me, but left me to be driven out,
proclaimed an exile! You might say that the city only granted
what I myself had asked for, but it was not so. For on that day,
when my soul was seething and Hades* seemed sweetest to me,
I wanted to be stoned to death, but no one stepped forward
to fulfill my desire. As time passed my torment mellowed,
and I realized that my rage at my former errors had been excessive.
Yet after all that time the city still drove me from its land,
and those sons who could have helped their father
were not willing to do so! Without so much as a word from them

*God of the underworld.

I was left an exile and a beggar, to roam forever.
It is only these two girls, mere maidens, who nurture me
and keep me alive, in so far as their nature will allow,
who see that I wander protected, and who provide me
the sustenance of family. As for the other two,
they have preferred to the man who begot them a throne,
a ruling scepter, and a king's sway over the land.
But they shall never gain me as an ally, nor shall they benefit
from ruling Thebes! I know this from the oracles
of which this maiden has told me, and from weighing
the ancient prophecies that Apollo has fulfilled for me.
So let them send Creon or some other man who wields power
in Thebes. Strangers, if you are willing to watch over me,
together with the guardian goddesses of this community,
you will gain a great protector for this city, and strife for my
enemies.

CHORUS

You are worthy of pity, Oedipus, both you
and your daughters. And since you speak
of becoming the protector of this land,
I wish to offer you some counsel.

OEDIPUS

My dearest friend, you are my host, and I shall do all that you bid.

CHORUS

You must now perform purification rites
for the deities on whose ground you first trod.

OEDIPUS

How must I do that? Tell me, strangers.

CHORUS

First, bring sacred water from the eternal fountain,
and touch the water with purified hands.

OEDIPUS

And once I have touched this untainted water?

CHORUS

You will find some bowls there, the work of a skilled craftsman.
Form a wreath around the rims and handles.

OEDIPUS

A wreath of twigs or woolen threads?

CHORUS

You must use lamb's fleece, freshly shorn.

OEDIPUS

I shall do that. But how shall I conclude the rite?

CHORUS

Stand facing the first light of dawn and pour the libation.

OEDIPUS

Must I pour from the dishes of which you have spoken?

CHORUS

Yes, three libations from each dish, emptying the dish with the last.

OEDIPUS

What must I mix into the libation? Tell me that too.

CHORUS

Water and honey. But do not add wine.

OEDIPUS

And when the black-leaved earth receives it?

CHORUS

With both hands lay down three times nine olive twigs
upon the ground, and utter this prayer—

OEDIPUS

Yes, I want to hear this. It is most important.

CHORUS

—that, as we call the Eumenides the Kind Ones,
they should receive the suppliant with kindness.
Ask this of them yourself or have another ask for you—
with hushed voice, one must not call out aloud to them.
Then leave without turning back. If you do this
I can stand beside you with conviction, otherwise
I would be in dread both for you and for me, stranger.

OEDIPUS

My daughters, do you hear what our hosts in this land have said?

ANTIGONE

We have heard. Command us, and we shall do what must be done.

OEDIPUS

I myself cannot go. I lack strength and sight,
two evil afflictions. One of you must go
and perform these rites. I believe
that one living soul with a pure disposition
can make this offering for myriad others.
Hurry, but do not leave me alone: my body
does not have the strength to move forward
abandoned and without a guide.

ISMENE *[to the CHORUS]*

I shall go perform the rite.
But tell me where I must do this.

CHORUS

Beyond the grove, maiden. If you lack anything,
there is a man living there who will tell you what to do.

ISMENE

I shall do this. Stay here, Antigone,
and guard our father. When one must toil

for a parent, one must not consider it toil.

[Exit ISMENE]

CHORUS

It is terrible to wake
what has long slumbered, stranger.
Yet there is something I yearn to know. 468

OEDIPUS

What?

CHORUS

The dreadful and unshakable suffering
that confronted you.

OEDIPUS

In the name of hospitality, 472
do not lay bare my cruel suffering.

CHORUS

It is such an infamous tale that it will not fade, stranger,
but I wish to hear the truth.

OEDIPUS

Alas! 476

CHORUS

Tell me, I beg you.

OEDIPUS

Woe, woe!

CHORUS

Tell me. After all, I granted everything you asked of me.

OEDIPUS

Strangers, I endured the greatest evils. 480
I endured them, as Apollo will bear witness,
yet none were of my own doing.

CHORUS

But how?

OEDIPUS

The city enmeshed me 484
in an evil marriage, which was my ruin.

CHORUS

Was it with your mother, as I have heard,
that you shared your infamous marriage bed?

OEDIPUS

Woe, stranger, it is death to hear this. 488
And these two are my—

CHORUS

What are you saying?

OEDIPUS

—my children, a two-fold curse—

CHORUS

O Zeus! 492

OEDIPUS

—who were born through the pains of a mother, both mine and theirs.

CHORUS

So they are your daughters and—

OEDIPUS

—also sisters of their own father.

CHORUS

Woe! 496

OEDIPUS

Woe! Myriad evils descend on me once more.

CHORUS
You have suffered indeed.

OEDIPUS
I have suffered unendurable torments.

CHORUS
But it was your doing.

OEDIPUS
It was not my doing.

CHORUS
What do you mean?

OEDIPUS
After my service to Thebes
I was given a gift that I, miserable wretch,
should not have accepted.

CHORUS
But tell me, unfortunate man, did you not—

OEDIPUS
What? What is it you want to know?

CHORUS
—kill your father?

OEDIPUS
Alas! You deal me a second blow, wound upon wound.

CHORUS
You have slain.

OEDIPUS
I have slain. But I have—

CHORUS
What?

OEDIPUS

—something to say in my defense.

CHORUS

What?

OEDIPUS

I will explain. Had I not killed him
he would have killed me. Before the law
I am guiltless. I did not know who he was.[4]

[Enter THESEUS]

CHORUS

But here comes our king, Theseus, son of Aegeus,
summoned by your claim.

THESEUS

I recognize you, son of Laius, for over the years I have often heard
how you ravaged your eyes in blood. And from what I was told
coming here, I surmised that it was you. Your garb and wretched face
assure me that it is you, unfortunate Oedipus, and, pitying you,
I ask what request you present to this city and to me,
you and the unfortunate companion at your side.
Tell me, for you would have to speak of a dreadful fate
to make me draw back. I have not forgotten that, like you,
I was raised a stranger, and that in strange lands
I faced mortal dangers like no other man.
So I would never turn away from protecting a stranger
such as you. I know that I am just a man,
and have no greater share in tomorrow than you do.

OEDIPUS

Theseus, in the few words you have uttered, your noble nature
has left little for me to say. You have spoken my name correctly
and that of my father, as well as that of the land

from which I have come, so there is nothing further to say 536
but what I desire, and that will be all.

THESEUS
Tell me, so I will know.

OEDIPUS
I have come to present you with my miserable body.
Its form is nothing, but its benefits 540
will far exceed any beauty.

THESEUS
What benefits do you allege you are bringing?

OEDIPUS
You shall learn that, but not now.

THESEUS
When will what you are offering be revealed? 544

OEDIPUS
When I die and you bury me.

THESEUS
You are asking for life's last rites, but you have forgotten
or count as worthless all that comes before.

OEDIPUS
For me, what I am asking embraces that as well. 548

THESEUS
It is a slight favor you are requesting.

OEDIPUS
And yet watch out! The conflict, I warn you, will be great.

THESEUS
Does this have to do with your sons or with me?

OEDIPUS
My sons will attempt to take me with them by force. 552

THESEUS

But if they want you to return, there is no need for you to remain in exile.

OEDIPUS

And yet when I wanted to stay in Thebes, they ignored my wish.

THESEUS

What madness! Anger brings no advantage when you are beset by evils!

OEDIPUS

Let me first explain everything to you, and then advise me. 556

THESEUS

Yes, explain. I do not want to form a judgment before you have spoken.

OEDIPUS

I have suffered terrible evils upon evils, Theseus.

THESEUS

Are you speaking of the old misfortunes of your family?

OEDIPUS

No, that is something every Greek knows. 560

THESEUS

Then what unbearable anguish are you suffering?

OEDIPUS

This is how it is with me. I was driven from my city
by the sons I engendered, but I am never to return
as I am the killer of my father. 564

THESEUS

How can they take you back to Thebes if you must not enter the city?

OEDIPUS
Apollo's pronouncement compels them.

THESEUS
What affliction do they fear from the oracle?

OEDIPUS
That they will be struck down by your city.

THESEUS
How will hostility arise between myself and them?

OEDIPUS
Dearest son of Aegeus,* it is only for the gods
that there is no old age or death: the rest is effaced
by all-powerful Time. The strength of the land
will decay and the strength in man's body will decay,
but loyalty too will perish and disloyalty thrive.
The same spirit does not endure between men who are friends,
or between one city and another. For some sooner,
for others later, a pleasant friendship will turn sour
but then become sweet again. If now the sun
between you and Thebes is shining, then Time
will give birth to countless nights and days
in which for a trifle this harmony will be shattered by spears.
If Zeus is still Zeus, and his son Apollo's oracles are right,
then my cold corpse, buried and asleep, will drink
their warm blood. But since it is not proper to divulge words
that must not be spoken, allow me to stop where I began.
I only ask you to stay true to your pledge that you will never say
you welcomed Oedipus to this land in vain.

CHORUS *[to THESEUS]*
My Lord, this man has shown that he is ready to fulfill
this promise and more for our land.

---

*Legendary king of Athens.

THESEUS

Who would reject the kind disposition of such a man?
Our cities' long-standing alliance makes him ever welcome
at our hearths. He also comes here a suppliant to the divinities,
bringing no small tribute to this land and to me.
I respect this, and so will never reject the benefits
he brings to us, and will have him dwell as a citizen in our land.

[To the CHORUS]

If the stranger pleases to stay here, I shall appoint you
to guard him, or he can come with me.
The choice is yours, Oedipus, I shall concur.

OEDIPUS

O Zeus, grant good fortune to men such as these.

THESEUS

What would you prefer? To come to my home?

OEDIPUS

If it were right for me to go, I would prefer that. But this is the place where—

THESEUS

Where you will do what? I shall not oppose it.

OEDIPUS

Where I shall vanquish those who drove me into exile.

THESEUS

The gift of your presence which you have spoken of is great.

OEDIPUS

If you will keep your pledge in exchange for mine.

THESEUS

Trust the man standing before you. I shall not betray you.

OEDIPUS
I shall not bind you with an oath as if you were untrustworthy.

THESEUS
You would not gain more by my oath than by my word.

OEDIPUS
How will you proceed?

THESEUS
What is it that you fear?

OEDIPUS
Men will come.

THESEUS
These men here will see to them.

OEDIPUS
You must protect me, for should you leave me—

THESEUS
You need not instruct me what to do.

OEDIPUS
A man filled with fear cannot hold back.

THESEUS
My own heart is untouched by fear.

OEDIPUS
You do not know the threats that have been made.

THESEUS
I know that no one
will carry you away from here against my will.
Threats often bluster with vain words of rage.
But once the mind regains control, the threats vanish.
I know that those who boldly spoke menacing words
about seizing you will find the voyage here long and hard sailing.

So take heart, for it was Apollo who has brought you here,
though I too pledge my help. Even if I am not present,
my name will protect you from suffering harm.

[Exit THESEUS]

CHORUS

You have come, stranger,
to a land of beautiful horses,
to sun-bright Colonus,
the sweetest
dwelling place on earth,
a place where nightingales
sing a soft lament
among the wine-dark ivy
in the green glades of the grove
of the god in which none may tread.
Here copious fruit
is sheltered from sun and winter winds,
here Bacchic Dionysos
treads the ground, attended
by the divine nymphs who nursed him.
In sun-bright Colonus
under the heavenly dew
the gold-gleaming crocus
and the beautifully clustered
narcissus abound,
the ancient crowns
of the two great goddesses.
The unstained water
of the sleepless streams of the Cephisus*
flow over the ample-breasted plains,
bringing nimble fertility to the crops.

---

*Sacred river that irrigates the plain west of Athens.

The choruses of the Muses
or Aphrodite of the golden reins
never turn from this land.
And there flourishes
in our land a plant
unknown in all of Asia
or on the Dorian island of Pelops,*
a tree not planted by human hand
but one that resprouts on its own,
a terror to the spears of enemies:
the gray-leaved olive,
nurturer of children.
No ravaging hand of man
in youth or old age
can destroy it,
for it is watched over
by ever-seeing Zeus Morios
and gray-eyed Athena.
And I have praise for another gift
that a great god gave our mother city,
a supreme honor for our land
of beautiful horses and colts
and beautiful sea.
O son of Kronos, Lord Poseidon,
you who enthroned our city
with this supreme honor,
for it was you who on our roads
first invented the horse-taming bridle
and on our sea
the ships' well-crafted oars
that fly to the rhythm

*The Peloponnese.

of the Nereids'* hundred feet.

ANTIGONE

O land most praised and honored!
Now you must turn your shining words into deeds!

OEDIPUS

What has happened, my daughter?

ANTIGONE

Creon is approaching, Father, and not without an escort.

OEDIPUS

My dearest elders, on you now my salvation depends.

CHORUS

Take heart, you will be saved. Though I am old,
the power of this land has not aged.

[Enter CREON]

CREON

Noble citizens of this land, I see in your eyes
that my arrival has sparked a sudden fear.
Do not be alarmed; do not utter evil words.
I have not come to take action, as I am an old man
and know this is a city that in Greece is illustrious
in power. I have been sent, despite my age,
to persuade this man to follow me back
to the land of Thebes. I was sent not by one man,
but urged to come by all our citizens,
since my kinship to Oedipus has led me
to mourn his torments more than any others in Thebes.
Hear my words, unhappy Oedipus, and come back home!
All Thebes justly summons you, I myself above all others!
I would be the most evil among men were I not to grieve

---

*The Nereids are daughters of Nereus, an old sea god; they dwell in the sea with their father.

at the ills that have befallen you, seeing you wandering
in misery like this through foreign lands, aged man,
with this girl attending you. Alas, the unhappy girl!
I would never have thought she could fall into such depths,
always caring for you in the state you are in,
at her tender age living like a beggar,
without knowing marriage, here for any man to seize.
Is this not a terrible reproach that I level at you,
at myself, and our entire family?
One cannot hide what is so clear!
By the gods of your forefathers, come back, Oedipus,
be persuaded to bid this city a kind farewell and return
to your own city and the house of your ancestors.
Your home deserves to be foremost in your respect,
for it nurtured you all those years.

OEDIPUS

You, who hold back from nothing, would cloak
the craftiest scheme with honest reasoning!
Why are you doing this? Why are you trying
to enmesh me once more in a snare
that would be so painful to me?
In the past, when I suffered the evils that descended
upon my house and it was my sweetest longing
to be expelled from Thebes, you refused me the favor!
But once my rage had slackened,
and remaining at home became sweetest to me,
you cast me out and exiled me. The kinship
you now speak of was not then so dear to you!
And now too, when you see this city and all its kin
embracing me in friendship, you try to drag me away,
saying harsh things in soft words. What is this delight
in being kind to men against their will?
It is as if one were to beg someone for something,
but he gives you nothing, refusing every help.

It is only once one is sated that he grants
what had been asked for, when his favor is no longer a favor.
Is not such a benefit meaningless? And can this not be said
about what you are now offering me,
things that are good in word but evil in deed?
I shall explain it also to these men, so I can show
how evil you are. You have come to take me away,
but not to bring me home!
You intend to leave me outside Thebes so that Thebes
can be delivered from harm coming from this land.
But you shall not have your way!
This is what you shall have instead: my avenging spirit
will dwell here in this land forever, and may my sons
attain only enough of Thebes' earth to die on.
Do I not understand better than you
what is taking place in Thebes? Much better,
for I have heard the truth from Apollo and his father,
Zeus himself. You have come here with honed tongue,
but you will garner more evil than good.
I know I cannot convince you with what I say,
so leave, and let us live here. I will not be living badly,
as I will be contented with my life.

CREON

Who do you think will suffer greater misfortune
from what you are saying and doing, you or me?

OEDIPUS

I would be happiest if you failed to convince me or these men.

CREON

Ill-fated man! Even with the passing years you seem not
to have acquired any sense, but disgrace your old age with filth.

OEDIPUS

You have a wondrous tongue, but I know of no just man
who can talk well on every subject.

CREON

It is one thing to speak much, and another to speak to the point. 768

OEDIPUS

As if your words have been brief and to the point!

CREON

I could hardly be brief and to the point with someone who has a mind like yours.

OEDIPUS

Leave! And I speak for these men too!
Do not stand guard over me where I am to live. 772

CREON

I appeal to these men, not to you, to witness
how you reply to a kinsman. If I should seize you—

OEDIPUS

But who could seize me, with all these allies at my side?

CREON

Even if I should not, you will still suffer pain. 776

OEDIPUS

With what action are you threatening me?

CREON

Of your two daughters, I have already seized one
and had her taken away. Now I shall carry off the second.

OEDIPUS

Woe! 780

CREON

You shall soon have more reason to lament.

OEDIPUS

You have my daughter?

CREON

And I shall have the other one before long.

OEDIPUS

Oh, my friends, what will you do? Will you abandon me
and not drive this impious man from your land?

CHORUS *[to CREON]*

Leave at once, stranger! None of your actions,
present or past, have been just.

CREON *[to his attendants]*

It is time to drag this girl off, if she is not willing to go.

ANTIGONE

Alas, miserable wretch that I am! Where can I flee?
What gods can help me, what mortals?

CHORUS *[to CREON]*

What are you doing, stranger?

CREON

I shall not touch this man, only the girl who is mine.

OEDIPUS

Lords of this land!

CHORUS *[to CREON]*

Stranger! What you are doing is not right!

CREON

It is!

CHORUS

How can it be?

CREON

I am only taking what is mine!

OEDIPUS

O city, save us!

CHORUS

What are you doing, stranger? Let her go,
or you shall feel the power of my blows.

CREON

Keep away!

CHORUS

Not from you, if those are your intentions.

CREON

If you harm me, you will have war with my city.

OEDIPUS

Did I not say as much?

CHORUS

Release the girl at once!

CREON

Do not command where you have no power.

[CREON hands ANTIGONE to his attendants]

CHORUS

Let her go, I tell you!

CREON *[to his attendants]*

And I tell you: take her and leave!

CHORUS

Come quickly, all you citizens! Hurry! Hurry!
Our city is being destroyed, my city is being violated!
Come quickly, I beg you!

ANTIGONE

They are dragging me away! Help me, strangers, help!

OEDIPUS

Where are you, my child?

ANTIGONE

I am being dragged away.

OEDIPUS

Reach out your hand to me, my child!

ANTIGONE

I do not have the strength.

CREON

Take her away!

OEDIPUS

Oh misery, misery!

[Exit ANTIGONE and attendants]

CREON

You will never again wander with those two staffs to lean on.
If you want to destroy your country and your friends,
at whose order I have come here though I am king,
then do your worst. I know that with time you will realize
that neither what you did nor what you are doing now
has been good for you. You have always been prone
to give in to your rage, despite the entreaties
of your loved ones, which has always been your ruin.

CHORUS

Stop where you are, stranger!

CREON

I warn you, do not touch me!

CHORUS

I shall not let you go, as you have robbed us of the maidens.

CREON

Then you will soon pay a price to my city
greater than those two girls.

CHORUS

What are you thinking?

CREON

I shall seize him and take him with me too.

CHORUS

Those are terrible words!

CREON

I shall take him now,
unless the king of this land chooses to stop me.

OEDIPUS

What shameless words! You would dare lay hands on me?

CREON

Be silent, I tell you!

OEDIPUS

May the goddesses of this place
not take away my voice before I utter
one more curse, you evil villain,
violently snatching from me my beloved eyes,
lost to me now like the others were.
May Helios, the all-seeing sun, grant that you
and your offspring have an old age like mine!

CREON

Do you see this, citizens of this land?

OEDIPUS

They see both you and me, and they know that I
defend myself with mere words against your actions.

CREON

I shall not restrain my anger, but will drag him away by force,
though I am now alone and weakened by age.

OEDIPUS

Oh misery, misery!

CHORUS

What audacity, stranger, if you think you can accomplish this.

CREON

I believe I can.

CHORUS

Then I will no longer consider our city a city.

CREON

Even a weak man will vanquish the great if he has justice on his side.

OEDIPUS

Do you hear what he is saying?

CHORUS

He will not achieve this, Zeus be my witness!

CREON

Zeus knows that I will, though you do not.

CHORUS

What hubris!

CREON

It is hubris, but you will have to endure it.

CHORUS

Help, citizens! Hurry!
Lords of the land, come quickly! Come!
This man has gone too far!

[Enter THESEUS]

THESEUS

What is all this shouting? What is happening?
What panic has led you to interrupt my sacrifice of oxen

at the altar of the Sea God, protector of Colonus? Tell me
why I had to rush here faster than my legs could bear with ease.

OEDIPUS

My dearest friend, for I recognize you by your voice,
I have suffered terrible things from this man!

THESEUS

What terrible things? Who has harmed you? Speak!

OEDIPUS

Creon, whom you see before you, has taken my only two children!

THESEUS

What did you say?

OEDIPUS

You have heard what I have suffered.

THESEUS

Attendants, run to the altars as fast as you can!
Summon all, those with horses and those without!
They are to leave the sacrifices and ride at full gallop
to where the two roads meet, so the maidens
will not leave our lands, and I, outdone by force,
be made a mockery of by this stranger!
Go, do as I command! Quickly!

[To CREON]

As for this man, if my anger was what he deserves,
he would not escape my hands unscathed.
He will now face the same law, exactly the same law,
that he brought with him. You will not leave this land
until you have returned the maidens and presented them
to me. Your actions have shamed me, have shamed
your forefathers and your country. You entered a city
that practices justice and reaches no decision without law.

Yet slighting the authorities of this land, you have forced
your way here to seize and carry off what you desire.
You seem to think that there are no men in my city,
that it is filled with slaves, that I am worth nothing! 892
And yet I am certain it was not Thebes
that raised you to be so evil.
Thebes is not known for rearing unjust men.
Nor would Thebes praise you if it knew 896
that you were robbing me of what is mine
and robbing the gods of what is theirs,
carrying off their miserable suppliants.
I would never set foot in your land and seize 900
someone without permission of the ruler,
whoever he may be, even if I had every right.
I would know how a stranger must comport himself
in another land. You are disgracing your city, 904
which does not deserve this, and the years
that make you old are emptying your mind.
I have told you already, and tell you again:
have the maidens brought here immediately, 908
unless you wish to become an inhabitant of this land
by force, against your will.
My words come from my mind as well as my tongue.

CHORUS

Do you see what pass you have come to, stranger? 912
Judging by your origin you seemed a just man,
but your deeds have shown you as evil.

CREON

Son of Aegeus, I did not think this city was devoid of men,
nor have I acted without thought, as you are saying. 916
In my actions I felt certain that none of your citizens
would have such zealous consideration for my kin that they
would stand with them in violent defiance against me.
I was convinced that your citizens would not receive a man 920

who had killed his father, a man proven impure
in an incestuous marriage that bore offspring.
I knew that the Council of the Areopagus of this land[5]
does not allow such transgressors to remain within the city.
Firm in my belief, I seized my prey, which I would not have done
had this man not uttered bitter curses against me and my
offspring.
I thought it fit to pay back the offence in this way,
for anger knows no old age. It is only the dead
who are not afflicted by pain. Hence do what you will.
Though what I say is just, I am alone, and that renders me weak.
But old as I am, I shall seek to repay you for your actions!

OEDIPUS

What shameless conceit! Whose old age
do you think you are disgracing, yours or mine,
when your mouth casts at me the murder, marriage,
and wretchedness that I in my misery bore against my will!
It was what pleased the gods, who may have harbored
some ancient wrath against my family. As for myself,
you cannot reproach me with any sin that I had to pay for
by committing those crimes against myself and my kindred.
Tell me this: if the oracles ordained that my father
would die by the hand of a son, how can you accuse me,
who was not yet conceived or begotten?
And if I was born to misery, as I was,
and came to blows with my own father, killing him
without knowing what I was doing and to whom,
how can you censure me for a deed that was unwitting?
As for my mother, are you not ashamed, you wretch?
She was your own sister, and you force me
to speak of her wedding as I now must?
Since you have gone so far with your profane utterance,
I cannot remain silent. She bore me, yes,

she bore me unknowingly—alas what evil!—
neither of us knew, and after bearing me
she bore my children, to my shame. But one thing
I know for certain: you speak ill of her and me with intent,
while I was compelled unknowingly into marrying her,
as you are now compelling me to speak of it.
I will not be called evil on account of this marriage,
nor on account of slaying my father,
for which you constantly reproach me bitterly.
Answer me just one question: if someone here,
this instant, were to try and murder you—
you, the just man—would you first enquire
if the murderer might perhaps be your father,
or would you make him pay immediately?
I believe that if you love your life
you will punish the culprit, and not stop
to weigh if it is just. Those were the evils
into which I was drawn, led by the gods,
and I believe that my father's spirit, if alive,
would not contradict me. But you,
who are not a just man, consider it fine to say anything,
utterable or unutterable, and taunt me with these reproaches
before these men. You consider it fine to flatter Theseus
to his face and extol Athens as well-governed. but while
you utter all this praise, there is something you have forgotten:
that if any land knows how to worship the gods with true reverence,
it is this land. And yet it is from this land that you
have tried to seize me, a suppliant and an old man,
laying hands on me and dragging away my daughters.
Thus I now call on the goddesses in supplication,
I beseech them with prayers, to come to my aid,
so that you will learn what kind of men protect this city.

CHORUS

The stranger, my king, is a good man. His fate
has been dire, but he merits our protection.

THESEUS

Enough words! The offenders are in flight,
while we, the offended, are standing here.

CREON

But what command do you have for a helpless man?

THESEUS

You will take me to the maidens. I and no other will be your escort,
as I know that you would not have permitted yourself your audacity
without the support of others. It is clear that you relied on arms
when you acted thus. I must respond to this. I will not let my city
become as weak as a single man. If the maidens are somewhere
in our land, then you will show me the place yourself. If the abductors
have fled with them, then we can save ourselves the labor
and others will hasten after them. Your men will not escape
to thank the gods in prayer. Lead the way! And remember
that the captor has been captured: fate has caught you, the hunter,
for what is seized unjustly through cunning cannot be kept.
Do you understand, or are my words as futile as whatever good words
were spoken when you were plotting this?

CREON

Nothing you say to me here can be faulted.
But when we return to our city, we shall know what to do.

THESEUS

Utter all the threats you want, but march forward!
As for you, Oedipus, remain here at your ease,
assured that unless I die, I will not rest
until I return your children to your care.

OEDIPUS

I bless you, Theseus, for your nobleness
and for the just concern you have shown us.

[Exit THESEUS, CREON, and attendants]

CHORUS

If only I could be
where enemy will soon turn upon enemy
and clash with Ares' bronze
by the shores of Pythian Apollo,
or the torch-lit shores
where the divine goddesses
nurse solemn rites for mortals
whose tongues have been silenced
with a golden lock
by the ministering Eumolpidae.
It is there, I believe, amid battle cries
that within our lands
belligerent Theseus
will soon rescue the two virgin sisters.
Or perhaps they are approaching
west of the snowy rock
from the pastures of Oea,*
fleeing on steeds,
racing in speeding chariots.
The enemy will be vanquished.
Terrible is Ares' imminent design,

---

*A plain between Athens and Thebes.

and terrible the might of Theseus
and his men. Bridles are flashing,
horsemen are riding
in full gallop,
they who honor Athena,
the goddess of horses,
and the Sea God
who girdles the earth,
the beloved son of Rhea.[6]
Will they act or are they biding their time?
For I foresee
that the maidens
who have suffered so terribly,
who have endured such terrible
strife from their own kin,
will soon return.
Zeus will do this today,
this very day.
I prophecy a propitious battle.
How I wish I were a dove
flying swiftly as the wind,
fast as the storm, my eye
peering down at the battle
from the lofty clouds!
O Zeus, all-seeing,
all-ruling supreme leader of the gods,
and venerated daughter of Zeus,
Pallas Athena! Grant
that the Athenians,
the guardians of our land,
will be mighty enough to seize their prey.
And I call upon Apollo the Hunter,
and his sister* who pursues

---

*Artemis, the huntress.

thick-spotted deer, to come to the aid
of this land and its people.
O wandering stranger, you will have no cause to say
that he who stood watch over you was a false prophet,
for now I see an escort bringing the maidens back.

[Enter THESEUS, ANTIGONE, ISMENE, and attendants]

OEDIPUS
Where, where? What are you saying? What did you say?

ANTIGONE
O Father, Father,
if only one of the gods could grant that you could see
this foremost of men who has brought us back to you!

OEDIPUS
My children! Are you both here?

ANTIGONE
The hands of Theseus and his dearest attendants have saved us.

OEDIPUS
My daughters, come to your father and let him
embrace you, who have returned beyond all hope.

ANTIGONE
We grant your wish, for we long for the favor we are granting.

OEDIPUS
Where are you? Where?

ANTIGONE
Here we are, Father.

OEDIPUS
My beloved daughters.

ANTIGONE
To a father every child is beloved.

OEDIPUS
You are my staffs!

ANTIGONE
The ill-fated staffs of an ill-fated man.

OEDIPUS
I have regained what is most beloved to me.
I would not be the most wretched man were I now
to die with you at my side. My children, steady your father,
huddle close to him, and comfort me who was made so desolate
and miserable by the distress of your abduction.

[To ANTIGONE]

Tell me what happened as briefly as you can,
since in a girl your age a few words should suffice.

ANTIGONE
This is the man who saved us. He must tell you the tale, Father.
That is how brief I shall be.

OEDIPUS *[to THESEUS]*
Dear friend, do not be surprised that I have spoken so long
and with such vigor to my children, who have reappeared
so unexpectedly. I know that I have you to thank for my rejoicing in them,
for it was you, and no other mortal, who rescued them.
May the gods grant what I desire for you and this land!
Among all men I have found only in you true fairness,
justice, and forthright truthfulness. With the blessing
I have just voiced I am repaying you,
as what I have I have through you and no other mortal.
Stretch out your right hand to me, my Lord,
so I may touch it, and, if custom will permit, kiss your face.
But what am I saying? How can a man born to misery
like me want you to touch someone within whom every stain
of evil exists? I will not allow it, nor can I wish it.

Only mortals who have experienced such evil
can share in it. I greet you as you stand there! 1108
May you always take care of me as justly as you have up to now!

THESEUS

I am not surprised that you spoke so long
in delight at your daughters, nor that you received
their words before mine. This does not offend me at all. 1112
I do not seek to make my life glorious through words,
but through deeds. The proof of this, venerable elder,
is that in all I pledged to you I did not break my word.
For here I am, having brought back the maidens alive, 1116
untouched and unassailed. As for how the battle was won,
why should I boast, when these maidens can tell you all?
But tell me what you think about something I heard
as I was coming here. It is a small matter, 1120
but it does warrant surprise, and one must never
consider anything beneath one's concern.

OEDIPUS

What is it, son of Aegeus? Tell me,
since I do not know what you are asking. 1124

THESEUS

They say that a man who is not from your city,
and yet is a kin of yours, has prostrated himself
as a suppliant at the altar of Poseidon at which
I was sacrificing when I set out to come here. 1128

OEDIPUS

Where is he from? What has led to his supplication?

THESEUS

I know only that he wants to speak briefly to you, as they
tell me,
about something of no particular importance.

OEDIPUS

About what? His being at the sanctuary can be of no small importance.

THESEUS

They say he only asks to speak to you
and then to be allowed to leave in safety.

OEDIPUS

Who can this suppliant be?

THESEUS

Is there anyone of your kin in the city of Argos
who might want to ask you a favor?

OEDIPUS

Stop, dearest friend!

THESEUS

What worries you?

OEDIPUS

Do not ask me to—

THESEUS

To do what? Tell me.

OEDIPUS

I know from what you are telling me who the suppliant is.

THESEUS

Who can he be that he should deserve my blame?

OEDIPUS

He is my son, O King, a son I hate. To listen to his words
would be more painful than listening to the words of any other man.

THESEUS

But surely you can listen without having to do what you do

not want?
Why should it be painful for you to hear him?

OEDIPUS

His voice is most hateful to his father.
Do not force me to grant this concession.

THESEUS

His being a suppliant might constrain you to concede.
Consider your duty of respect to the god.

ANTIGONE

Father, let me persuade you. Though I am still young
I offer this advice. Appease the king's mind
and grant the god's wish, and also accede
to your daughters: allow our brother to come.
He surely cannot force your resolve with any words
he might speak against what is right for you.
What harm is there in listening to mere words?
Deeds devised for evil are betrayed in speech.
You gave him life, so even if he has committed
the most evil and impious crimes against you, Father,
it is not right for you to pay him back in kind.
Let him come. Other men have evil sons
and burn with anger, but, admonished by their friends,
their passion is assuaged. You must look to the past,
not the present, and weigh the evils you have suffered
because of your father and your mother.
If you do, I know that you will understand the evil
that evil anger engenders. Deprived as you are
of your unseeing eyes you have powerful proof of this.
Give in to our entreaties. It is not good
that those who seek what is just must entreat you.
Nor is it good that you, a man who is being treated
so well, would not know how to requite it.

OEDIPUS

My child, the king and you have won me over with your words,
though what is pleasant to you is to me grief. I yield
to what pleases you all. But, my Lord, if that man
is to come here, let no one ever gain power over my life.

THESEUS

Venerable elder, you need speak these words but once,
not twice. I do not wish to boast, but rest assured
that you will be safe while the gods protect me too.

[Exit THESEUS]

CHORUS

He who is not content
with his moderate share
and seeks a longer span of life
is a great fool.
For the many long days
will gather up every kind of grief.
When man is dealt a life
that is longer than is good,
happiness is nowhere to be found.
Death the deliverer
brings an equal end to all,
the destiny of Hades
rising without nuptial song,
without lyre, without dance:
death is the end.
Not to be born is the condition
that surpasses all others.
But once man is born,
the next best thing is to return
with utmost haste to where he has come from.
For even youth with all its airy thoughtlessness
finds that ample suffering

is never far away.
What hardship is not at hand?
Murder, sedition, strife, battle, anger.
And then comes disparaged and
abhorred old age, infirm and friendless,
the most evil of evils gathered together.
That is the fate
of this unhappy man before us,
not mine alone, to be battered
by waves from all sides
like a north shore in a winter storm.
He too has been battered
by relentless waves of doom,
waves that come from where the sun sets,
from where the sun rises,
from where its midday rays shine,
waves that come from the distant Rhipe Mountains
that are immersed in night.

ANTIGONE

But here comes the stranger, I think.
He has no escort, Father, and tears
are streaming from his eyes as he approaches us.

OEDIPUS

Who is he?

ANTIGONE

The man who has occupied our thought so long.
Polynices is here.

[Enter POLYNICES]

POLYNICES

Alas, what am I to do? O sisters! Should I first shed tears
for my own misfortunes, or for those of my aged father
I see before me? I find him with you in a strange land,

an outcast and in rags. Ancient repulsive grime
has mingled with this ancient man, rotting his body,
and on his eyeless head tangled hair is ruffled by the wind.
And just as wretched are the scraps of food he carries
to fill his wretched stomach. Have I, miserable as I am,
learnt all this too late? I proclaim that in caring for you, Father,
I have been the worst of men! Ask no one else what I am,
hear the truth from my own lips. And yet,
just as Mercy shares the throne with Zeus in all his deeds,
let Mercy also stand with you, Father! My past errors
cannot increase, but they can be remedied!
Why are you silent?
Say something, Father! Do not turn away. Will you not answer me?
Will you send me away in silence, without explaining your wrath?
My sisters, you who are this man's daughters, will you not try
to move our father's unapproachable and unaddressable lips
so he will not send me away in dishonor, me, a suppliant
under the protection of the god, send me away without replying,
without speaking a single word!

ANTIGONE

O miserable Polynices, tell him yourself
what it is you seek. A long speech that will cause
either delight or anger, a speech that will spark pity,
can sometimes give voice to those who are voiceless.

POLYNICES

As your advice is good, I shall speak. But first
I shall call upon the god himself to stand by me,
the god from whose altar the king of this land
told me to rise and come here, and granted me the right
to speak and receive an answer, before leaving in safety.
I want the same assurance from you, strangers,

and from my father and my sisters.
Father, let me tell you why I have come.
I have been driven into exile from the land of my forefathers
because as your first-born I claimed the right to sit
as king upon your throne. It was for this that Eteocles,
though younger in birth, drove me from Thebes.
He did not vanquish me through word, battle,
or deed, but managed to persuade the city.
All this, I say, has been caused by your Furies,
as I have also heard from the soothsayers.
I made my way to Dorian Argos and secured
King Adrastos as my father-in-law. Then I made allies
of all those considered foremost in the land of Apis,
men honored for their prowess. With them
I gathered an army of the Allied Seven to march on Thebes,
to drive my brother from my land or die in a most righteous cause.
That said, why have I come? I have come, Father, to beg you
as a suppliant for myself and my comrades-in-arms
whose seven companies, whose seven spears, have now
surrounded Thebes: one is lance-hurling Amphiareus,
foremost in valor of war and reading the auguries of birds.
The second is Aetolian Tydeus of the House of Oeneus.
The third, Eteocles, is an Argive by birth. Fourth
is Hippomedon, sent by his father Talaus. The fifth is Capaneus,
who boasts that he will raze the Theban citadel to the ground.
Sixth is the Arcadian Parthenopaius, named after Atlanta,
who remained a virgin until she finally conceived her trusted son.[7]
And then there is me, your son, or if I am not your son
but born to an evil destiny, yet called your son by all—
I lead this fearless Argive army on Thebes.
We all beg you, Father, as suppliants, by your daughters
and by your life! Abandon your wrath in favor of my cause

as I march out to seek vengeance against my brother for
casting me
into exile and robbing me of the city of my forefathers.
For if one is to believe the oracles, the side that you join
will prevail. In the name of our sacred fountains
and the gods of our race, I beg you to hear me and yield,
for we are outcasts, beggars and strangers:
you are a stranger here too. Since destiny has doled out
the same fate for both of us, you and I must live fawning on
others.
And that arrogant tyrant back in Thebes, O misery,
laughs at us both. But if you stand by me in my venture
I shall destroy him swiftly and with ease.
Then I shall drive him out by force
and restore you to your palace once again,
and restore myself too.
If you desire these things as I do I shall prevail,
but without you I shall not emerge unscathed.

CHORUS

Out of respect for our king who sent this man, Oedipus,
answer him, and then let him depart.

OEDIPUS

Guardians of this land, had Theseus not sent this man
to me, deeming it proper for this man to hear me speak,
then he would never have heard my voice.
He shall depart having been granted this concession,
but he will hear things from me that will not brighten his life.

[To POLYNICES]

It was you who cast me out, most evil villain,
when you held the Theban scepter and throne
that your brother now holds, it was you who cast out
his own father, banished him to exile, reduced him
to the rags that spark your tears, now that you face

the same miseries as I. But there is no cause for tears!
While I live I shall bear my fate, remembering you
as my murderer. It was you who fed me this torment,
who cast me out, who sent me wandering and begging
for my daily sustenance. Had I not begotten
these two girls who feed me, had I relied on you,
I would not be alive. It is they who protect me,
they who nurse me. They are men, not women,
when it comes to shouldering my burdens.
You are not my sons, you are the sons of another!
A god is watching over you, but not as he will
when your army marches on Thebes. You will never
destroy Thebes, but will fall, tainted with blood,
as will your brother. These are the curses
I have brought down upon you in the past
and which I now summon to my side
to make you and your brother respect your begetter,
even if the father who begot you is blind.
These daughters have stood by me.
My curses will vanquish your supplication
and your throne, if Justice, so named of old,
is still seated at the side of Zeus,
according to the ancient laws!
Leave! I, who am no longer your father,
spit on you, most evil of evil villains!
And take with you the curses
I have called down upon you!
You and your army will not conquer your native land,
nor will you ever return to the plains of Argos!
You will be slain by your brother's hand,
just as you shall slay him who drove you out.
That is how I curse you! I summon the paternal gloom
of Tartarus to house you, I summon the goddesses,
I summon Ares, who has locked you and your brother
in this terrible hatred. You have heard this, now go,

and tell all the men of Thebes and all your trusted
comrades-in-arms
that these are the honors Oedipus bestows upon his sons.

CHORUS

Polynices, I do not take pleasure in the paths
you have chosen. You must leave at once.

POLYNICES

Alas for my path, alas for my failure, alas
for my comrades-in-arms. What will be the end
of our march from Argos—O misery!—an end
I cannot reveal to any of my comrades.
Nor can I turn back. I must face my fate in silence.
Sisters and children of this man! As you hear
the harsh curses our father has pronounced,
I beg you by the gods that if these curses
should be fulfilled, and you have managed to return home,
do not dishonor me, but bury me in a tomb
with all the funerary offerings. The praise
you have gained through your sufferings
for our father will grow, and not be diminished
by the service you will have done me.

ANTIGONE

Polynices, I beg you to listen to my plea.

POLYNICES

Dearest Antigone, what is it, tell me.

ANTIGONE

Turn your army around and march it back to Argos at once.
Do not destroy yourself and Thebes.

POLYNICES

That is impossible. How can I
march the army back if I show such fear?

ANTIGONE

My brother, why must you unleash your wrath once more?
What gain is there in razing to the ground the city of our fathers? 1380

POLYNICES

It is shameful to be an exile, and for me,
the older brother, to be mocked by the younger.

ANTIGONE

Do you not see how you are fulfilling our father's prophecies,
which proclaim that you will kill one another? 1384

POLYNICES

But that is his wish. Must we not abide by it?

ANTIGONE

O misery! But who will dare follow you
after they have heard the prophecies our father has spoken?

POLYNICES

We shall not announce the bad news, for a good commander 1388
will proclaim what is good, not that which will dishearten.

ANTIGONE

So you are determined, my brother?

POLYNICES

I am, you must not hold me back.
I have to set out along this path, ill-fated 1392
and evil as our father and his Furies have made it.
But may Zeus grant you and Ismene all that is good
if you will do for me in death what you cannot do in life.
Let me go, my sisters, and farewell, 1396
for you will never look upon me again.

ANTIGONE

O misery!

POLYNICES

Do not lament.

ANTIGONE

Who would not lament, dear brother,
seeing you set out for Hades, looming before you?

POLYNICES

If I have to, I shall die.

ANTIGONE

No, you must not! Do as I beg you!

POLYNICES

Do not beg me when you must not.

ANTIGONE

What misery,
to be deprived of you!

POLYNICES

It is for divine fate
to turn out one way or the other. I pray to the gods
that you and Ismene never come to evil.
All know that you do not deserve ill fortune.

[Exit POLYNICES. A peal of thunder.]

CHORUS

New evils are coming
from somewhere new, grave new evils are coming
from the blind stranger, unless fate
is striving toward some end,
for I cannot call any decision of the gods futile.
Time sees, Time sees all things always,
one day toppling some,
the next making others rise.
O Zeus! The sky is thundering!

OEDIPUS

My children, my children, is there anyone here who can
bring to me Theseus, in every way the best of men?

ANTIGONE

Why are you summoning him, Father?

OEDIPUS

This is the winged thunder of Zeus
that will carry me to Hades. Bring Theseus here at once!

[A peal of thunder]

CHORUS

Did you hear that! A great, ineffable thunder
sent down by Zeus is resounding,
and fear rushes through my limbs.
My soul cowers in terror. Lightning
is again flashing through the sky!
What can this mean? Will Zeus
hurl his thunderbolt? Oh dread!
He never casts it in vain or without disaster.
O great sky! O Zeus!

OEDIPUS

My children, the foretold end of this man's life
has come. There is no turning away.

ANTIGONE

How do you know? What leads you to think this?

OEDIPUS

I know it for certain. But someone must quickly
go to bring here the king of this land.

[A peal of thunder]

CHORUS

Ah! Ah! There! Again!
A piercing sound engulfs us.

Mercy, O god! Mercy, if you are to bring
darkness to our Mother Earth!
May I find you favorable
when you come upon me,
and may I not be rewarded with harm
for having looked upon this accursed man!
Lord Zeus! To you I call!

OEDIPUS

Is Theseus near? My daughters, will he
still find me alive, and my mind clear?

ANTIGONE

Why are you anxious that your mind be clear?

OEDIPUS

I want to grant the favor that I pledged
for his treating me with kindness.

CHORUS

O! O! Theseus my son, come, come!
Come, even if you are at the edge
of the hollow sacrificing oxen at the altar
of Poseidon of the sea!
The stranger wants to grace you
and the city and his friends with a just favor
because he was treated well.
Hurry, our King, come quickly!

[Enter THESEUS]

THESEUS *[to the CHORUS]*

What is this clamor rising from you all,
from you citizens, and as I now see from the stranger too?
Was it a thunderbolt from Zeus or a shower of crashing hail?
Anything can be expected when a god sends down such a storm.

OEDIPUS

O king, I yearned for your appearance, and one of the gods
has granted your path good fortune.

THESEUS

What is happening, son of Laius?

OEDIPUS

The scales of my life are falling, and I wish to die,
having kept my promises to you and the city.

THESEUS

What sign has convinced you that your end is near?

OEDIPUS

The gods themselves are the heralds who announce it to me,
they do not fail any of the allotted signs.

THESEUS

How have they revealed this to you, venerable elder?

OEDIPUS

The incessant thundering of Zeus and the many bolts
that flash from his invincible hand.

THESEUS

You convince me. I have seen you prophecy much,
and it has all come true. Tell me what must be done.

OEDIPUS

Son of Aegeus, I shall explain to you the things
that will be secured for your city, untouched
by the ravages of time. I will now lead you to the place
where I must die, lead you without the help of any guide.
You must reveal to no one where this place is hidden,
where it lies, so that it will always render you more protection
than shields or allied spears. As for those things
that are hallowed, and which even words must not rouse,
you will learn them yourself when you go there alone.

I will not reveal them to any of these citizens,
not even to my children, though I love them.
You must always guard these things, and when you
reach the end of your life, divulge them only
to the foremost man of this city, who must then
throughout the ages each time divulge them to his successor.
This way the city in which you live will never be destroyed
by the Sown Men, for myriad cities, though governed well,[8]
can turn to reckless insolence, and the gods can see clearly
—though late—when their divine laws are abandoned for
madness.
You, son of Aegeus, must never fall into such error.
But I am saying these things to a man who already knows them.
We must now go to that place, for the presence of the god
is hastening me. We must not linger. My daughters,
follow me, for I now shall prove your guide,
just as the two of you used to guide your father.
Come, but do not touch me: I alone must find
the sacred tomb where it is fated that I shall be buried.
Here, this way, follow me! Hermes, the guide,
and the Goddess of the Underworld are leading me.
O lightless sunlight, you have been mine,
but this is the last time my body shall feel you!
I will now go to Hades to shroud the ending of my life,
and you, dearest of strangers, may you, your land,
and your attendants be blessed. When I am dead
remember me in your everlasting good fortune and prosperity.

[Exit OEDIPUS]

CHORUS

If the laws permit me
to revere the unseen goddess with prayers
and you, Lord of those immersed
in night, Aidoneus,
Aidoneus, I pray

that the stranger may reach
without anguish, without doom,
the all-concealing plains of the dead
down below in the House of Styx.*
After the many and futile torments
that beset him,
a just god will now exalt him.
O Goddesses of the Earth!
O unconquered body of the beast,
untamed Guard of Hades
who lies at the gates of the underworld,
whimpering from your cave,
welcoming strangers.
O son of Earth and Tartarus!†
I pray that you will free the path
for the stranger descending
to the plains of the underworld.
To you I call, Eternal Sleep!

MESSENGER

Men of this city, in a few words
I could tell you that Oedipus is dead.
But I cannot describe so briefly
what took place, nor were the events brief.

CHORUS

The poor man is dead?

[Enter MESSENGER]

MESSENGER

Know that he has departed from this life!

---

*In the underworld.

†Another name for the underworld.

CHORUS

How? Did divine fate grant that the unhappy man die without pain?

MESSENGER

It was indeed most miraculous! How he left from here
you know, as you were present: his daughters and friends
did not guide him—it was he who led us all.
But when he reached the precipice, the Bronze Threshold
rooted in the earth with brazen steps, he stopped
at one of the many paths that branch out by the valley
where the covenant of Theseus and Perithous is honored.[9]
He stood between the valley and the Thorican Rock,
and then sat down between the hollow pear tree
and the stone tomb. He loosened his filthy garments,
calling to his daughters to bring him water
from whatever stream they might find,
so that he could cleanse himself and pour libations.
The maidens went to the hill of verdant Demeter
which was in sight and swiftly carried out his wishes,
bathing and clothing him as is the custom.
But once everything he desired had been provided
and everything he asked for fulfilled, Zeus thundered
from beneath the earth and the maidens trembled,
falling at their father's knees, weeping
and beating their breasts. When he heard
their long and bitter laments he embraced them,
and said, "My children, from this day forth
you will no longer have a father.
Whatever you had to do for me is now over.
You will no longer be burdened with the task
of tending me. It has been hard for you, my daughters,
I know. But all this is softened by a single word: love—
and no one has given you love more than I.
Yet you must live the rest of your lives without me."

Thus they wept, clinging to one another. Then
their lamentations and sobs ceased and there was silence.
But suddenly a voice called out to Oedipus,
and our hair stood on end in terror.
A god kept calling, from different places:
"Hey! You! Oedipus! Why are you lingering!
You are delaying our departure!"
When Oedipus realized that it was a god calling to him,
he bade Theseus, the king of our land, to come to him,
and, once the king had approached, said to him:
"My dearest friend, clasp the hands of my daughters
in ancient pledge, and you, my children,
clasp the hands of Theseus! Promise that you
will never knowingly betray these maidens
and that you will forever and with care
do what will be best for them."
Without lament, Theseus, noble in nature,
gave his word to the stranger, and then Oedipus
touched his children with unseeing hands and said:
"My daughters, you must bear this with noble mind.
You must leave this place and not insist on seeing
or hearing what divine law forbids. Leave in haste.
Only King Theseus must remain and know what will take place."
We all heard these words, and wept streams of tears
as we led the maidens away. We walked a distance,
and after a short while turned around and saw
that Oedipus was no longer there.
We only saw our king, shading his eyes
as if something terrible had appeared, unbearable
to behold, and then saw him bowing down in silence
to the earth and to Olympus of the gods.
No mortal but Theseus knows by what doom
Oedipus perished. No fiery bolt of lightning
destroyed Oedipus, nor had a storm risen from the sea.
A guide sent by the gods must have come for him,

or perhaps the dark foundation of the underworld opened
to embrace and welcome him, for he left without lament
or pain, in circumstances most miraculous.
And if what I say strikes anyone as foolish,
I will not try to convince him that I am not a fool.

CHORUS

Where are the maidens, and their friends who are escorting them?

MESSENGER

They are nearby. The sound of lamentation
signifies that they are returning here.

[Enter ANTIGONE, ISMENE, and attendants]

ANTIGONE

Alas! Alas! It falls to us—it falls to us to lament
not only this woe, but all the woes of our father's
accursed blood that flows in our veins, wretches that we are,
blood for which in the past we endured
prodigious and never-ending pain,
and now we must take with us the torments
beyond belief that we have seen and suffered.

CHORUS

What took place?

ANTIGONE

Dear friends, we can only guess.

CHORUS

Has he gone?

ANTIGONE

He has gone, gone just in the way
one would most desire: for neither Ares
nor the sea clashed with him,
but the land hidden beneath

engulfed him, carrying him away
to a mysterious doom.
O misery! A deadly night
will now weigh down our eyes,
for how can we find sustenance
for our lives, so hard to bear, as we roam
through distant lands and face the swells of the sea?

ISMENE

I do not know how we can!
May murderous Hades
engulf me so that I, poor wretch,
may share my aged father's death!
The life awaiting us is not to be lived.

CHORUS

Best of children, you must nobly bear
what the gods will send you.
Do not burn with grief. No one can fault
the path that you have chosen.

ANTIGONE

I marvel how at times we yearn for sorrows,
for what was in every way a torment to me
was no torment when I was at my father's side.
Father, dear Father,
now forever wrapped in darkness beneath the earth!
Even down there, you will never
be unloved by me and my sister.

CHORUS

In the end, he—

ANTIGONE

In the end he accomplished what he desired.

CHORUS

What did he desire?

ANTIGONE

He died in this strange land,
as was his wish, and now he lies
in a bed that is forever
gently shaded, he lies mourned
and lamented: my eyes, Father,
weep tears, nor can I eradicate
my great sorrow!
Alas, you desired to die
in a strange land and so
died without me at your side.

ISMENE

Oh misery! What destiny
awaits me and you, dear sister,
without our father?

[Two lines missing in the Greek text]

CHORUS

Dear maidens, since he sacredly resolved
the end of his life, you must no longer grieve.
No one is beyond the reach of evils.

ANTIGONE

Sweet sister, let us hurry back up this path!

ISMENE

Why should we do that?

ANTIGONE

I long so much to—

ISMENE

What?

ANTIGONE

—to see that abode beneath the earth.

ISMENE
What abode?

ANTIGONE
Oh misery! Our father's!

ISMENE
But that is against divine law! Do you not understand that—?

ANTIGONE
Why do you rebuke me? 1680

ISMENE
Because it is not right, but also—

ANTIGONE
Also what?

ISMENE
He descended to Hades without a tomb
—neither of us were there.

ANTIGONE
Take me there, and slay me where he disappeared. 1684

ISMENE
Woe, woe! What misery!
How will I then live my ever-wretched life,
alone and without means?

CHORUS
Dear maidens, do not be afraid. 1688

ANTIGONE
How will we escape?

CHORUS
But you already have—

ANTIGONE
What do you mean?

CHORUS

—escaped a fate that would have turned out badly.

ANTIGONE

There is a thought that worries me.

CHORUS

What is this thought?

ANTIGONE

I do not know how we can return home.

CHORUS

You must not even try!

ANTIGONE

We are victims of strife.

CHORUS

You have been victims of strife before.

ANTIGONE

Sometimes inescapable, sometimes even worse.

CHORUS

A great sea of strife has been your lot.

ANTIGONE

Alas! Alas! Where can we go, O Zeus!
Toward what hopes will divine fate impel me?

[Enter THESEUS]

THESEUS

Do not weep, my children. One must not mourn
those to whom the dark night beneath the earth
is a favor granted by the gods. The gods would resent it.

ANTIGONE

Son of Aegeus, we kneel before you in supplication.

THESEUS
What is the request you want me to grant, my children?

ANTIGONE
We want
to see for ourselves the tomb of our father.

THESEUS
But divine law prohibits this.

ANTIGONE
What do you mean, lord and king of Athens?

THESEUS
Oedipus himself has forbidden me
ever to approach the sacred tomb that holds him
or to tell any mortal where it lies.
He said that if I keep this pledge,
my land will forever remain free of woe.
The son of Zeus, Orkos, the god of oaths
who hears all, heard my pledge.

ANTIGONE
If that is our father's wish,
then we shall accept it.
But send us to ancient Thebes,
so we can try to prevent the murder
that is descending upon our brothers.

THESEUS
I shall do this and everything else
that will help you and will prove a favor
to the man newly departed, who now lies
beneath the earth. I shall not fail in my efforts.

CHORUS
Do not weep and do not break into laments.
For these things
are now unalterable in their authority.

ANTIGONE

CHARACTERS

ANTIGONE	daughter of Oedipus and Jocasta
ISMENE	Antigone's sister
CHORUS	of Theban citizens
CREON	king of Thebes, brother of Jocasta
GUARD	
HAEMON	son of Creon
TIRESIAS	a blind prophet
A MESSENGER	
EURYDICE	wife of Creon

Non-speaking

Guards

Attendants

[Outside the palace gates. Enter ANTIGONE and ISMENE.]

ANTIGONE

My dear Ismene, sister, my flesh and blood,
ah, what further evils springing from Oedipus
will Zeus send us while we two are still alive?
Among the evils that have afflicted you and me
there is nothing painful or without ruin I have not witnessed,
no disgrace and no dishonor. And what is this new edict
that Creon has recently proclaimed to all the people of the city?
Have you heard? Do you know of this?
Or has it eluded you that our enemies' evil designs
now turn toward our loved one?

ISMENE

No news, either sweet nor painful,
has reached me, Antigone, since we were robbed
of our two brothers, who died in a single day by each other's hand.
Since the Argive army fled tonight I know nothing more,
neither auspicious nor menacing.

ANTIGONE

I was aware of that, and so I called you to come
outside the courtyard gate, so you alone would hear.

ISMENE

What is it? I see you are brooding over something you want to tell me.

ANTIGONE

Yes, for Creon has given one of our brothers a burial
and left the other unburied and dishonored.
Creon has treated Eteocles with justice, they say,
burying him beneath the earth and honored
among the dead below. As for the wretched body of Polynices,
they say an edict has been proclaimed to all citizens

that none may lament over the body or cover it with a tomb.
The body must remain unwept, unburied, a welcome booty
for birds in search of meat to feed on. That, they say,
is what worthy Creon has also decreed for you and me,
yes, for me as well. And he is coming here to proclaim this
in no uncertain terms to whoever does not know it.
He considers it no slight matter: anyone who transgresses
in this matter is to die by public stoning.
That is how things stand, and you will soon reveal
if you are of noble nature or base, though nobly born.

ISMENE

What can I do, my long-suffering sister?
If this is the way things are, how can I help
by unraveling or tightening the knot?

ANTIGONE

You must consider whether you will join in the labor and the deed.

ISMENE

What dangerous deed are you thinking of?

ANTIGONE

Are you prepared to join hands with me to raise the dead body?

ISMENE

You mean to bury him, though it has been forbidden to the city?

ANTIGONE

Yes, I do. I will not betray my brother and yours,
even if you yourself are not willing to help.

ISMENE

My reckless sister! This, despite Creon's prohibition?

ANTIGONE

He has no right to keep me from my own.

ISMENE

Alas! Think, sister, how Father perished,
despised and shamed as a result of the wrongs
which he himself uncovered, raising his hand against himself, 48
tearing out his eyes. Then his mother and wife,
a double title, destroyed her life with twisted cords.
And thirdly, our two brothers slain in a single day,
each raising a murderous hand against the other 52
in a common, wretched fate. Just think,
now that the two of us are left alone, how miserably
we shall perish if we go against the decree and power of the king
in violation of the law. We must not forget that we were born women, 56
unfit to battle men, and also that we are ruled by those more powerful,
and must obey this command and others harsher still.
So I ask for forgiveness from those beneath the earth,
since I am compelled in this by those in authority, and must obey. 60
Acting beyond our power makes no sense.

ANTIGONE

I will not urge you, even if I somehow could.
I do not want you to act with me. Do what you think best.
I shall bury him myself. In doing so I shall die a noble death. 64
I shall lie, beloved, with my beloved brother, having committed
a pious crime, since the time I must please those below
is far longer than the time I must please those here above.
I shall lie below forever. As for you, if you think it best, 68
then hold in dishonor the things honored of the gods.

ISMENE

I am not dishonoring them, but it is not in my nature
to act against the will of the citizens.

ANTIGONE

You may make those excuses, but I
shall raise a tomb for my dearest brother.

ISMENE

Alas, poor sister, how I fear for you.

ANTIGONE

You need not fear for me. Set out a straight path for yourself.

ISMENE

But at least do not reveal your deed to anyone.
Keep it secret, as I shall.

ANTIGONE

Oh go ahead and proclaim it! You'll be more hateful
if you keep silent and do not announce it to all.

ISMENE

You have a burning heart for chilling deeds.

ANTIGONE

But I know I am pleasing those I must please most.

ISMENE

If you have the strength—but you desire the impossible.

ANTIGONE

Well, once my strength fails I shall cease.

ISMENE

But to begin with, it is wrong to strive for the impossible.

ANTIGONE

If you say this, you will be reviled by me
and justly hated by him who is dead.
But leave me and my ill counsel to suffer a dreadful fate,
for nothing is greater than a noble death.

[Exit ANTIGONE, away from the palace]

ISMENE

Go, if that seems best to you, but know
that even though you will commit a foolish deed,
your loved ones truly love you.

[Exit ISMENE, into the palace. Enter CHORUS of Theban elders]

CHORUS

Ray of the sun,
the most beautiful
light to shine upon Thebes
of the Seven Gates,
you have appeared at last,
eye of golden day,
rising above the streams
of our River Dirce,
sending into flight
the white-shielded man
who had come from Argos
in full panoply, piercing him
sharply with your shining bridle.
Incited against our land
by Polynices' petulant quarrels,
he swooped over our land like an eagle,
with shrill shrieks, snow-white wings,
myriad weapons, and helmets
bearing great horse-hair crests.

He hovered over our houses,
threatening us with murderous spears,
encircling the mouths of our seven gates.
But he was forced to turn away
before his jaws were filled with our blood,
before Hephaestus'* pinewood torches

---

*Hephaestus is the god of fire.

could devour our wreath of towers,
for such clamor of battle
did Ares* incite behind him
that the dragon's opponent could not prevail.

Zeus detests the boasts
of an arrogant tongue,
and seeing the enemy marching on us
in a mighty stream, with the haughtiness
of flashing gold, he hurled
his brandished fire at the man
who was too quick to shout victory
high on our ramparts.

The man staggered and fell to the ground
with a resounding crash, he who,
torch in hand, had been reveling
in crazed and frenzied onslaught,
breathing blasts of harsh and hostile winds.
The battle had turned against him,
the great god Ares with hard blows
doling out deadly fates.

Seven captains then took position
at the seven gates, equal facing equal,
leaving their bronze weapons
in homage to Zeus, bringer of victory.[1]
Only the two miserable brothers,
who though born of one father and one mother,
leveled against one another
spears of equal power,
inflicting a common death.

---

*God of war.

But Victory, bringer of glory,
has arrived, rejoicing with a zeal
equal to that of chariot-rich Thebes.
So let us forget the recent wars,
and proceed to all the temples of the gods
with night-long dancing, and may Bacchus*
who shakes the earth of Thebes be our leader.

[Enter CREON and his attendants]

But here comes the king of our land,
Creon, the son of Menoeceus,
through the will of the gods
the city's new ruler after the late events.
What thoughts are gathering in his mind
that made him call together
by public proclamation
this special assembly of elders?

CREON

Men of Thebes! The gods who have tossed our city on tumultuous
waves have once more restored it to a safe course.
Hence I have summoned you through messengers,
separately from all the rest, because I know
that you revered the power of Laius' throne,
and then that of Oedipus when he ruled our city.
And when Oedipus came to ruin you still continued
with unwavering spirit to be true to his sons.
Since they have perished in a single day
in a twofold fate, each striking the other
in polluting fratricide, it is I now,
by right of kinship to the dead, who hold the power
and the throne. It is impossible to understand
a man's heart and judgment until he has proven himself

*A.k.a. Dionysos, god of the wild and of tragedy.

in governing and lawmaking.
For I believe and have always believed
that whoever does not hold to the best decisions
in ruling a city but out of fear keeps his tongue in check,
is the basest of men. And I have even less esteem for a man
who deems a friend more important than his fatherland.
May Zeus the all-seeing be my witness,
but I would never remain silent at seeing destruction
instead of salvation advancing upon our citizens,
nor would I ever consider a man who is hostile
to this land my friend, since I know one thing for certain:
it is this land that keeps us safe. It is when we sail straight
that we make friends. Such are the laws
with which I shall make this city prosperous.
I have now issued edicts for the citizens
akin to these laws concerning the sons of Oedipus.
Eteocles, who perished fighting for this city, showing prowess
with his spear in battle, may be covered with a tomb
and honored with all the rites due the most noble of the dead.
But his fugitive brother Polynices returned from exile,
striving to torch and burn the land of his fathers
and the temples of our gods, and to feed on kindred blood,
leading the Thebans into slavery.
Therefore know that it has been proclaimed to the city
that no one may lament him or honor him with funerary rites,
but must leave his body unburied, so that all can see it devoured
by dogs and birds of prey. That is my decision.
I shall never hold evil men in higher esteem
than the righteous, but will honor any man,
dead or alive, who is well disposed to this city.

CHORUS

Son of Menoeceus, you have decided
that this is the just course for the man who is hostile
and the man who is well-disposed to this city.

It is in your power to use every law,
whether for the dead or for us who are alive.

CREON

See to it that my orders are carried out.

CHORUS

You should charge a younger man to bear such a burden.

CREON

I already have guards at hand to stand watch over the dead man.

CHORUS

Then what is the order that I am to carry out?

CREON

To stand firm against anyone who disobeys my edict.

CHORUS

No one would be foolish enough to seek death.

CREON

Death will indeed be the reward.
But hope of illicit gain will often ruin a man.

[A GUARD enters]

GUARD

My Lord, I will not tell you that I come to you out of breath,
after running all the way here as fast as my feet could carry me.
I did not. I stopped many times along the road to think,
and kept wanting to turn and head back the way I came.
You see, my head kept speaking to me, telling me things like:
"Miserable fool, why are you going there when you are bound
to be punished?"—"You wretch, why are you stopping again?
If Creon hears the news from someone else, you're sure
to feel his wrath!" Such thoughts went whirling through my head
as I slowly trudged on, making a long journey out of a very
short one.

But in the end, my resolve to come here and report to you
won the upper hand. Though the news I bring is in fact worthless
I will still report it, because I have come clinging to the hope
that I will suffer nothing except my proper fate.

CREON

What is it that frightens you?

GUARD

Let me speak on my own behalf: I neither did the deed,
nor did I see the doer. So it would be most unfair
for me to come to any harm.

CREON

I see you are taking every precaution, protecting yourself
on all sides. Your news must be worrying.

GUARD

Terrible things prompt much hesitation.

CREON

So will you finally speak! And then be off!

GUARD

Well, I shall speak. Someone buried the dead man
and then went away, after scattering dry earth on the corpse
and performing the necessary funerary honors.

CREON

What are you saying? Which of the men dared do that!

GUARD

I do not know. The ground was neither gashed by an axe,
nor were there any signs that there had been digging with a hoe.
The ground was hard and dry, and unmarked by wagon wheels:
whoever did this left no tracks. When the first sentry of the day
showed us what had been done, we were all struck with amazement.

The dead man had disappeared, yet he was not covered by a tomb
but by a light layer of earth, as if someone had been trying
to fend off a curse. There were no signs of a beast or dog
having passed or torn at the corpse. We began shouting evil things
at one another, one guard accusing the next, and it nearly ended in blows,
with no one there to stop us. Each man thought the other had done the deed,
but nobody could be shown to be guilty, every man proclaiming
he knew nothing. We were even ready to pick up hot irons
in our hands or to walk through fire and swear oaths by the gods
that we neither did the deed nor knew anyone who had done it
or who had it in mind to do such a thing. Finally,
since we had thought of everything with no result,
one of the men spoke words that made us all lower our heads in fear,
for we could not rebut him, nor see how we could save ourselves.
He stated plain and simple that the deed had to be reported
to you immediately, that it could not be hidden. This idea prevailed,
and the lot fell to me, the unluckiest of men, to deliver
this wonderful bit of news to you. So I have come here
against my wish to you who I am certain wishes I had not.
For I know how it is: nobody loves the bringer of bad news.

CHORUS

My Lord, for some time now I have been wondering
if this deed might not have come from the gods.

CREON *[to the CHORUS]*

Stop before your words enrage me and you prove yourself
a fool despite your venerable age! How can you suggest
that our divinities would show any interest in this corpse?

Did the gods bury him with special honors for being
such a great benefactor to Thebes, a man who came here
to torch their column-ringed temples and all the rich offerings,
a man who came to destroy both their land and their laws?
Do the gods honor evil men? No, they do not!
I know that some in this city find it hard to bear me
and have been mumbling against me behind my back,
shaking their heads, refusing to keep their necks
under the regal yoke, refusing to afford me
the veneration I deserve. And I am aware
that some will have been beguiled into doing this
through bribery. No baser custom ever arose among men
than money. It sacks cities and uproots men from their houses.
It is a masterful teacher in perverting the minds of just men,
inciting them to turn to disgraceful deeds.
Money has shown man how to give himself over to iniquity
and encouraged him to every impious deed.
Those who succumbed to bribery to do this deed
have ensured that they will pay the price.

[To the GUARD]

But as I still honor Zeus, I warn you—and I swear this upon my oath—
unless you and the other guards find out who buried the dead man
and bring me the perpetrator in person, Hades will not be your only reward.
You will be strung up alive until you reveal the details of this outrage!
That way you will learn the outcome of illicit profit and learn
that you must not seek to gain in any way. Disgraceful profit
has ruined many more men than it has saved.

GUARD

Will you allow me to say something, or must I leave without a word?

CREON

Do you not realize that you have already angered me by what you have said?

GUARD

Are you stung in your ears, or in your soul?

CREON

Why are you trying to locate where I am stung?

GUARD

The one who did this deed hurts your mind, but I hurt your ears.

CREON

Oh what a babbler you are!

GUARD

That I am, but still I did not do this deed.

CREON

Of course you did! You sold your soul for silver!

GUARD

Never!
How terrible when he who supposes supposes wrongly.

CREON

You can pun all you want on supposed supposings, but if
you do not bring me those who did this, you will recognize
to what extent dishonorable gain can bring misery.

GUARD

I hope he will be found, I really do! But whether
he is caught or not—and Fate will decide that—
you will never see me coming here again. I am saved,
without having hoped or expected to be,
and I owe the gods much gratitude.

[GUARD exits]

CHORUS

There are many wonders,
but none more wondrous than man.[2]
He crosses the gray seas
in wintry southern winds,
cutting through engulfing waves.
He tames Earth,
the most exalted of the gods,
the imperishable, the inexhaustible,
following his plow year after year,
as his tribe of horses furrows the soil.

He hunts and snares
with his meshing coils of net
the nimble-minded race of birds,
the tribes of savage beasts,
the creatures of the deep.
Skillful man!
With his clever tools
he masters the beasts
that roam the mountains,
taming the shaggy-maned horse
and bringing the vigorous bull under the yoke.

He has taught himself speech
and wind-swift thought,
the rules of tempered city life,
and ways to flee beneath the sky
the darts of hostile storm and frost.
He walks toward the future
with all his cunning.
It is only from Hades*
that he cannot devise an escape.

*God of the underworld.

But in counsel with his fellows
he finds flight from deadly disease.

He has inventive wisdom beyond measure,
and moves now to evil, now to good.
Weaving the laws of the earth
with the justice of the gods
to which he is under oath,
he stands in high honor in his city.
But the man who recklessly
transgresses against what is just
is banished from the city.
He who does such a thing
will not share my hearth
or my thoughts.

[The GUARD returns, leading ANTIGONE]

The extraordinary wonder I see before me
leaves me confounded! How can I deny
that this maiden is Antigone, whom I know so well?
O wretched daughter of a wretched father, Oedipus,
what is happening? Can they be bringing you here
for disobedience of the royal edict,
caught in an act of utter madness?

GUARD

She is the one who did the deed. We seized her
as she was burying the dead man. But where is Creon?

CHORUS

Here he is, coming back out of the palace.

CREON

What is it? What matter makes my arrival opportune?

GUARD

My Lord, a mortal must never swear an oath

that he will not do something, for second thoughts
often undo a man's former conviction.
I would hardly have returned here after your threats
that rattled me last time. But because powerful
and unexpected joy is greater than any other pleasure,
I have come here—even though I was bound
by oath not to—bringing this maiden, who was seized
as she was performing burial rites. This time
we did not cast lots, but Hermes* sent
this bit of luck to me and nobody else.
And now, my Lord, I hand her over to you:
question and examine her as you wish. As for me,
I am now released entirely from these evils.

CREON

How did you seize her? Where did you bring her from?

GUARD

She was burying the man. You know it all.

CREON

Do you understand what you are saying? Do you mean the words you are speaking?

GUARD

It was her I saw burying the corpse, though you forbade it.
Am I not speaking clearly and in plain words?

CREON

How was she seen? Was she caught in the act?

GUARD

This is how it happened. When we got back
after having heard those terrible threats from you,
we swept away the earth covering the dead man,

---

*Messenger god who links the earthly and the divine realms.

and laid the rotting body bare. We went to sit on top of a hill
with our backs to the wind, so that we would not be struck
by the stench, and kept our eyes open, goading each other
with threats so that none of us would slacken in our task
of guarding the body. We continued arguing
until the sun's dazzling disk reached the center of the sky
and the heat began to blaze. But suddenly a storm
whipped up a whirlwind of dust, an evil from above.
The dust covered the plain, ravaging all the foliage of the trees,
and filling the great wide sky. We shut our eyes and waited
for the divine ill wind to pass. It raged for a long time,
but when it settled down a girl appeared.
She let out the bitter cry of a bird that comes upon
the warm cradle of its nest robbed of chicks.
The maiden, seeing the uncovered corpse,
broke into lamentation and shouted evil curses
at those who had done the deed. She quickly
gathered dry earth, and, holding a well wrought amphora up high,
honored the dead man with a thrice-poured libation.
Seeing her, we ran and seized her, but she showed no fear,
and we questioned her about the previous and the present deeds.
She denied nothing, which for me was sweet,
but also painful: to have escaped these evils
is very sweet, but dragging a maiden, long known,
to her destruction is painful. But, as is natural,
all this matters less to me than my own survival.

CREON *[to ANTIGONE]*
And you I ask, you who hang your head to the ground,
do you admit or deny having done this deed?

ANTIGONE
I did the deed and do not deny it.

CREON *[to the GUARD]*
You can leave, and go wherever you like,
free of these heavy charges.

[Exit GUARD. CREON to ANTIGONE]

As for you, tell me—and keep to the point—
did you not know that there was a proclamation forbidding this?

ANTIGONE
I knew. How could I not? It was proclaimed clearly enough.

CREON
And yet you dared transgress my law?

ANTIGONE
In my eyes Zeus did not issue this edict,
nor did Justice, Dike, who dwells with the gods below,
set up such laws for man. I did not think your edicts
so powerful that you, a mortal, could overstep
the unwritten and unbending laws of the gods.
These laws are not a thing of today or yesterday,
but exist forever in eternity. No one knows when they appeared.
I am not prepared, from fear of one man's will,
to pay the penalty before the gods. That I would die some day
I knew well enough, even without your proclamation.
But if I die before my time, then I declare that death
will be my gain, for if one lives as I do,
beset by so many evils, dying can only be for the best.
Meeting such a fate is in no way anguish.
But I would have felt true anguish
had I left unburied the body of my mother's dead son.
My death will bring me no sorrow.
You might think I am acting foolishly,
but perhaps it is a fool who is charging me with folly.

CHORUS
The maiden's unyielding nature shows she was born

of an unyielding father. She does not know how to yield to evils.

CREON

And yet it is obstinate spirits that are most prone to fall.
How often do we see the sturdiest iron, baked hard by fire,
shatter and break into many pieces. I know that spirited horses
are disciplined by a bridle's tiny bit: one who is the slave of another
cannot be allowed to exult. And yet this maiden
knew well enough how to commit an outrage
by violating the laws that have been prescribed.
This now is her second outrage, for having done the deed,
she now boasts of it and ridicules us. By this, in truth,
it is not I who am a man—it is she who is a man
if she is allowed to wield such power unpunished.
Though she is my sister's child and closer kin to me
than any other of our family who have Zeus as protector,
she and her sister will not escape a most terrible death.
I blame Ismene equally for planning this burial.
Summon her immediately! I just saw her inside,
raging and bereft of her senses. The mind
of those hatching deceitful deeds in darkness
can be caught out like a thief, beforehand.
I hate those who, caught in evil deeds,
try to glorify them.

ANTIGONE

Do you want anything more than to seize and kill me?

CREON

I want nothing more. When I have that, I have everything.

ANTIGONE

Then why do you delay? For nothing in your words
pleases me, or ever will please me,
just as whatever I say will always displease you.
And yet where would I have achieved more prominence

and glory than by burying my own brother in a tomb?
And I say that all these men here would agree
if fear were not tying their tongues.
A king is fortunate in many ways, in particular
that he can do and say what he pleases.

CREON

You alone among these Thebans see things this way.

ANTIGONE

These men see it this way too, but they seal their lips before you.

CREON

Are you not ashamed to think differently from these men?

ANTIGONE

There is no disgrace in honoring one of my own flesh.

CREON

Was not the one who died battling him also of your blood?

ANTIGONE

Yes, of my blood, from one mother and father.

CREON

How then can you grant to one brother an honor that is a dishonor to the other?

ANTIGONE

The dead man will not testify to that.

CREON

He will, if you honor him equally with the impious one.

ANTIGONE

It was not a slave who died, but my brother.

CREON

He died while ravaging this land, while the other died defending it.

ANTIGONE
All the same, Hades demands these rites.

CREON
But the evil man does not deserve the same honor as the good.

ANTIGONE
Who knows if that principle is revered below.

CREON
An enemy is never a friend, not even when dead.

ANTIGONE
My nature strives for friendship, not for enmity.

CREON
When you descend to Hades you can love those you must love.
But while I live, no woman shall overrule me.

[Enter ISMENE]

CHORUS
But here is Ismene at the gates,
crying sisterly tears of love.
A cloud above her eyebrows
disfigures her flushed face,
wetting her pretty cheeks.

CREON *[to ISMENE]*
You have lurked inside my house like a viper,
secretly sucking my blood. I did not know
I was nurturing two plagues and two underminers of my throne.
Tell me, will you admit that you took part in the burial,
or will you swear that you knew nothing of it?

ISMENE
I have done the deed—that is, if Antigone will stand behind me.
I share in the blame and will bear the burden with her.

ANTIGONE

But justice will not grant you this. You were not willing
to act with me, nor I with you.

ISMENE

But I am not ashamed to share
your suffering amid your troubles.

ANTIGONE

Hades and those below will bear witness to whose deed this was.
I will not accept a friend who is a friend only in words.

ISMENE

Do not deprive me, sister, of the honor of dying with you
and paying my debt to the dead.

ANTIGONE

You cannot share in my death, nor try to make your own
what you did not touch. It will be enough for me to die.

ISMENE

What desire for life can I have if I am bereft of you?

ANTIGONE

Ask Creon. It is he you support.

ISMENE

Why do you hurt me this way, when it brings you nothing?

ANTIGONE

And yet I suffer while I mock you.

ISMENE

Can I not stand by you somehow, even now?

ANTIGONE

Save yourself. I will not hold your escape against you.

ISMENE
Alas, poor wretch that I am, will I fail to share your dreadful fate?

ANTIGONE
You chose to live, I to die.

ISMENE
Though not without giving you my reasons.

ANTIGONE
You appear right to these men, I appear right to others.

ISMENE
And yet our sin is equal.

ANTIGONE
Comfort yourself. You are to live, while my soul
perished long ago, which is why I could help the dead.

CREON
From what I see, these maidens have lost their senses:
one just now, the other at birth.

ISMENE
The senses we have, my Lord, might be lost
when we are in misery. They abandon us.

CREON
For you, anyway, who have chosen
to do evil things with those who are evil.

ISMENE
What kind of life is there for me, alone, without Antigone?

CREON
Do not speak of Antigone as though she were still here for you.

ISMENE
Will you kill your own son's bride?

CREON

There are enough other arable fields.

ISMENE

No other that is as fitting for him.

CREON

I hate bad wives for my sons.

ISMENE

O beloved Haemon, how your father dishonors you.

CREON

You anger me with your words of marriage.

ISMENE

Will you really deprive your own son of Antigone?

CREON

Hades will be the one to stop this marriage.

ISMENE

It seems that it is decided that Antigone will die.

CREON

It has been decided. Do not waste time.
Attendants, take them inside! From now on
these women must be kept under guard,
for even bold men will try to escape
when they see Hades approaching.

[Exit ANTIGONE and ISMENE with Creon's attendants]

CHORUS

Happy are they whose life has tasted no evil.
For those whose house is shaken by a god,
adversity will spread over the generations.
It will swell like a wave
whipped by the raging
sea winds of Thrace,

a wave that surges
over the deep and dark abyss,
raising up black sand as it crashes
against the echoing
wind-thrashed shores.

Ancient are the ills of the House of Labdacus.
I see the evils of their dead piling up.
One generation cannot set the next generation free
before a god strikes it down;
there is no respite.
A ray of light shone upon
the last sprouting bud of the House of Oedipus,
but again the bloody dust of the nether gods
has blighted it with crazed words
and the Furies* of the mind.

O Zeus, what transgression of man
can constrain your power?
Sleep that subjugates all cannot defeat it,
nor can the divine, untiring months.
O master, unaging throughout eternity,
you glory in the dazzling
splendor of Olympus!
In the past this truth stood firm,
and will stand firm
in near and distant days to come:
no mortal's life will long progress without ruin.

Far-roaming hope, though fortunate for some men,
deceives many others
with foolish desires.
Hope creeps up on the man who is unaware

*Deities of vengeance who pursue wrongdoers.

until he burns his foot in blazing flames.
A wise man once spoke
famous words: there is a point
when evil seems good to a man
whose mind a god is leading to ruin.
This man avoids ruin
for only the briefest time.

[Enter HAEMON]

Here is Haemon, last born of your sons.
Does he come grieving over the fate
of his betrothed Antigone, in anguish
over his thwarted marriage?

CREON

We will soon know better than the prophets could foretell.
My son, have you come in anger at your father
after hearing my edict on your intended bride,
or do you love us notwithstanding what we do?

HAEMON

Father, I am yours, and I follow
your wise counsel as you guide me.
I value no marriage more
than your good guidance.

CREON

My son, you must always be disposed this way
in your heart, and must stand behind
your father's judgment in all things.
This is why a man will pray to beget
and have in his house sons who will obey him,
who, like their father, would repay an enemy
with evil and afford a friend every honor.
What can you say about a man who begets
worthless sons, except that he has provided

hardship for himself and mocking laughter
to his enemies. My son, never cast aside reason
out of desire for a woman. Know that an evil woman
in your bed will prove a chilling embrace.
What greater wound can there be than an evil friend?
Spurn this maiden and cast her out like an enemy,
let someone in the House of Hades marry her.
She alone out of all our citizens was caught
committing disobedience for all to see!
Now I shall not prove false to Thebes, but will kill her.
Let her keep invoking Zeus, Protector of Kindred!
If I encourage my kin by blood to be unruly,
it would encourage unruliness outside my family all the more.
Only he who within his house is just will also appear
just in the city. But I shall not bestow my praise
on whoever transgresses the laws and does violence to them,
or seeks to impose commands on those who rule.
He whom the city appoints must be obeyed in matters
small and just, and also in matters large and unjust.
I would trust such a man to be a noble ruler and a good subject,
who, if ordered to stand in a hail of spears,
would stand firm, a just and brave soldier.
There is no greater evil than anarchy:
It destroys cities and lays waste to houses.
It causes routs in battle. But obedience,
following good guidance, saves many lives.
That is why decrees must be defended, and not left
to be undermined by a woman. If one is to be toppled,
then better by a man. May we not be called inferior to a woman.[3]

CHORUS

Unless our years mislead us, we deem that you are speaking wisely.

HAEMON

Father, the gods sow wisdom in man, the most valuable

of his possessions. As for me, I can neither say
nor would I take it upon myself to say in what way
your words might be wrong. And yet a view
other than yours might be correct as well.
You are not in a position to observe everything men say or do,
all those things with which they find fault, for to a simple man
your countenance is frightening when words are spoken
that you might not be pleased to hear. But I,
standing in the shadows, can hear what is being said in secret,
can see how the city mourns for Antigone. People are saying
that the maiden who least deserves such a fate is to die
in the most evil way for the most glorious deed.
She did not leave her brother unburied, her flesh and blood
who fell amid the slaughter, to lie exposed,
prey for dogs and birds ravenous for raw flesh.
Is she not worthy of golden honor?
Such black words are creeping through the city.
For me, Father, there is no treasure more valuable
than a father who thrives in good fortune.
What greater delight is there for a son than a father whose name
is held in high esteem, or for a father who can delight in his son.
So do not insist on only one idea, as if your word and no other
can be right. Whoever thinks that he alone has wisdom,
or has the gift of oratory and reason like no other, that man,
when held up to scrutiny, proves empty. It is no disgrace
for a man, even if he is wise, to continue learning
and not permit himself to become fixed and rigid.
One sees along rivers swollen by winter storms
that the trees that yield will save their branches,
while those that resist perish from root to crown.
Likewise, he who steers a ship, drawing the sail too taut,
leaving no slack at all, will find himself capsized
and sailing on with his benches under water.
So yield and let your anger subside. Be open to change.
If I, a younger man, may offer an opinion, then I say

that it would be ideal for a man to be born filled with knowledge.
But as he is not, by the usual tilt of the scales,
he should seek to learn from those speaking wisely.

CHORUS

My Lord, if Haemon's words are worthy, it would be good
for you to learn from him, and you, Haemon, from Creon.
You both have spoken wisely.

CREON

Are men of our age to be schooled by a man of his?

HAEMON

Not in anything that is unjust. I am young,
but I urge you to consider my deeds and not my age.

CREON

What deeds? Showing reverence to those who rebel?

HAEMON

I would not urge you to honor those who are evil.

CREON

Has that woman not been seized with that very sickness?

HAEMON

The people of Thebes say that she has not.

CREON

Is the city to tell me how I am to rule?

HAEMON

Do you not see that you are speaking like a child?

CREON

Should I rule this land for others and not myself?

HAEMON

There is no state that belongs to a single man.

CREON

Does the state not belong to its ruler?

HAEMON

Alone in a desert, you would make a perfect ruler.

CREON

I see that he is in league with a certain woman.

HAEMON

Only if you are that woman, for it is you that I care for.

CREON

You vile boy! You are questioning your father's justice!

HAEMON

Only because I see you offending justice.

CREON

Is it wrong for me to uphold my kingly powers?

HAEMON

You are not upholding them when you trample on honor due to the gods.

CREON

How abominable, bowing to a woman!

HAEMON

You will not find me bowing to what is shameful.

CREON

And yet every word you say is for that woman.

HAEMON

And for you, and me, and the gods below.

CREON

You will not marry her while she is alive.

HAEMON
Then she will die and, dying, destroy another.

CREON
You dare to go so far as to threaten me?

HAEMON
What threat is it to speak against empty judgments?

CREON
You will pay with bitter tears for daring
to teach me wisdom, though wisdom is what you lack!

HAEMON
Were you not my father, I would say it is you who is lacking in wisdom.

CREON
Slave to a woman! Don't provoke me with your prattle!

HAEMON
Do you wish to speak, and, having spoken, hear no answer?

CREON
Ha! Is that what I wish? Well, by Olympus,
know that you'll pay for this string of insults!

[To the attendants]

Bring that woman here, so that she may die this instant
near her bridegroom, before his very eyes.

HAEMON
No, never! She shall not die before my eyes,
nor will you ever look upon me again with yours.
Ply your madness with those friends willing to endure it!

[Exit HAEMON]

CHORUS
He ran off fired with wrath, my Lord.

At his age, it is hard for a heart to bear pain.

CREON

Let him do as he pleases. He can act and think thoughts above man's state,
but he will not save those two maidens from death.

CHORUS

Will you really go so far as to kill them both?

CREON

You are right. I will not kill the one who did not touch the dead man.

CHORUS

What manner of death are you planning for the other?

CREON

I will have her taken to a place deserted by people,
and shut up alive in a rocky cave. I will leave her only enough food
for me to avoid divine sacrilege and for the city not to be contaminated.
In that cave, begging Hades, the only one among the gods she reveres,
she might manage to elude death, or at least realize, albeit too late,
that it is pointless to revere those who are in Hades' realm.

CHORUS

Eros, undefeated in battle,
Eros, who devours man's possessions,
you who lie in wait at night
in the soft cheeks of a maiden,
you who fly over the seas,
over shepherds' huts!
None of the immortals can escape you,
nor can any ephemeral mortals.

Whoever is possessed by you is crazed. 756

You waylay the minds of just men,
dragging them to their ruin as they become unjust.
This quarrel you have sparked
among men of the same blood. 760
But it is Desire, triumphant as co-ruler
alongside mighty laws, that radiates
from the eyes of the beautiful bride.
The goddess Aphrodite,* invincible, 764
exults in her will.

[ANTIGONE enters, escorted by attendants]

At this sight, I too am transported
beyond the mighty laws.
I can no longer stem the fountain of tears 768
as I see Antigone approaching the chamber
that will bring her eternal rest.

ANTIGONE

You see me, citizens of my paternal land,
treading my final path, 772
beholding the last sunlight
I shall ever see.
Hades, who brings eternal rest,
is leading me alive 776
to the banks of Acheron,†
unmarried.
No wedding hymn
shall ever be sung, 780
for I shall be Acheron's bride.

---

*Goddess of love and sexual desire.

†River in the underworld.

CHORUS

But you depart for this crypt
of the dead with glory and praise,
unmaimed by withering disease,
not cut down by a sword.
It is by your own law,
alone and unique among mortals,
that you descend alive to Hades.

ANTIGONE

I have heard that the daughter of Tantalus,[4]
the stranger from Phrygia,
perished most sorrowfully on the peak
of Mount Sipylus. A rocky growth
embraced her like entangling ivy.
Men say that rain and snow
never leave her as she pines away,
always weeping, her valleys
wet with tears. Like her,
the god will lull me to sleep.

CHORUS

But she is a goddess begotten of a god,
while we are mortals born of man.
And yet what greater thing
can be said of a dying woman
than that she shares the fate of the divine
Both when she lives, and later when she dies.

ANTIGONE

Alas, you mock me!
By the gods of our fathers,
why do you abuse me,
who am not yet dead,
but standing before you?
O city, O foremost men of Thebes,

woe, O source of our River Dirce,
and sacred earth of chariot-rich Thebes!
You shall witness under what laws
I am to be led, unwept by friends,
to the strange vault
of my rock-entombed grave.
Woe, wretched me, neither among mortals
nor among corpses, not alive, not dead.

CHORUS

Proceeding to the limits of daring,
my daughter, you were thwarted
by the high throne of Justice,
and are now paying for the evils of your father.

ANTIGONE

You have touched on a most painful memory
of my father's threefold evil fate,
and the fate of all of us
who are descendants
of the illustrious House of Labdacus.
O woe, my mother's ill-fated marriage,
and my father's incestuous
coupling with his unfortunate mother,
which brought about my wretched birth!
It is to my kindred that I am going,
cursed and unmarried, to live at their side.
Alas, dear brother, your own marriage
was ill-fated, and in your death
you slew me, though I am still alive.

CHORUS

Your piety is virtuous indeed,
but he who holds power
will not tolerate it being defied.
It is your own self-willed nature that has destroyed you.

ANTIGONE

Unlamented, friendless, unwed,
my thoughts in turmoil, I am led
along my final path,
never again to see the eye of the sacred sun!
No tears are shed for my fate,
and none of my friends lament!

CREON *[to the attendants]*

Do you not know that if lamentation were to keep
impending death at bay, no one would cease lamenting?
Quickly, take her away as I have ordered
and seal her in her confining grave. Leave her there abandoned
and alone, to die or be entombed alive in her new abode.
I remain pure and blameless in this maiden's fate,
but whatever it may be, she shall be deprived
of the right to live among us.

ANTIGONE

O tomb, my bridal chamber, eternal abode
deep beneath the earth! I am descending
to my beloved kindred, all perished,
who have been received by Persephone among the dead.
I descend, the last of all, my death far more cruel than theirs,
coming before the fated term of my life.
But I am filled with hope that my father will receive me
with love, that I will be beloved to you, mother,
and beloved to you, my dear and very own brother.
For when you all perished it was I who washed
and adorned you with my own hands,
I who poured offerings on your graves.
And this is how I am rewarded, Polynices, for laying out
your body, though I honored you as is proper
according to wise custom. And yet had I become a mother
of children, or if a husband had died and lain rotting
above the ground, I never would have taken up such a burden

against the will of the people. What principle
has driven me to say this? If I had had a husband
and he had died, I could have found another,
and I could have had another child, had I been bereft of one.
But with my mother in Hades and my father too,
no other brother could sprout for me again.
That was the principle that led me to perform your burial,
sweet brother, for which Creon sees me as having transgressed,
for which he believes that I defied him with a dreadful act.
Now he is having me led away under guard, unmarried,
with no wedding hymn, without my share in marriage
or in raising children. Deserted by friends, ill-fated,
I descend alive into the cavernous vaults of the dead.
Why should I, wretched as I am, still look to the gods?
Which of the gods can I appeal to, when it was
through my pious act that I have been charged with impiety?
If this pleases the gods, then once I have suffered my doom
I will come to know my guilt. But if the guilt lies with my judges,
I wish for them no greater evil than the evil
they are unjustly inflicting on me.

CHORUS

The same gusts of passion
still possess her.

CREON

That is why those who are leading her away
will cry bitter tears for being so slow.

ANTIGONE

Alas, these words bring me closer to my death.

CREON

Do not hope that things will turn out any other way.

ANTIGONE

Land of Thebes, city of my forefathers
and ancestral gods,
I am being led away, I cannot defer it any longer.
Behold, nobles of Thebes,
the last of your Royal House!
Behold my suffering for my virtuous act
of piety at the hands of these men.

[Slow exit of ANTIGONE and attendants as the CHORUS addresses her for the last time]

CHORUS

Danae too suffered Fate's yoke,[5]
forced to relinquish heavenly light
for the darkness of a bronze-bound chamber.
O daughter, daughter, Danae too
was of noble birth
and was even cherishing within herself
the gold-streaming seed of Zeus.
But awesome is the power of Fate:
neither wealth, nor war,
nor tower or dark, sea-beaten
ship can escape it.

Fate also tamed the hotheaded son of Dryas,[6]
King of the Edonians, for his offensive
outburst of frenzied rage. He was confined
by Dionysos in a rocky prison so that the flaring power
of his terrible frenzy would fade away.
The son of Dryas came to know the god
after he had offended him in his frenzy
with his taunting tongue. He had sought to stop
the god-possessed Maenads* and their Dionysian fire,

*Women who celebrate Dionysos with frantic sound and dance.

and had angered the flute-loving Muses.

Beside the twin dark-blue seas of the Bosporus
lie the shores of the unwelcoming Thracian land
of Salmydessos. There the god Ares,
who was worshiped near the city,
saw the two sons of King Phineus
being dealt a hideous wound
by the king's wild wife.[7]
She inflicted blindness upon their eyes,
which now crave vengeance,
having been savagely struck
by her bloodied hands and sharp weaving shuttles.

Wasting away in desolate suffering,
the sons, born of an ill-wed mother, weep;
and yet she was of the ancient line of Erechtheus*
and daughter of the wind god Boreas,
raised in distant caves amid her father's stormwinds,
where she, a daughter of gods, roamed
the steep mountains swift as a horse.
But even she, my child,
was assailed by the eternal fates.

[Enter TIRESIAS, led in by a youth]

TIRESIAS

Lords of Thebes, this boy and I have walked here together,
two seeing with the eyes of one, for it is customary
that the blind walk this way with a guide.

CREON

What has happened, aged Tiresias?

---

*Mythical savior of Athens.

TIRESIAS

I shall inform you, and you must obey the prophet.

CREON

I have never distanced myself from your counsel.

TIRESIAS

That was when you were steering the city on a straight course.

CREON

I can testify to your help, as I have profited from your counsel.

TIRESIAS

Give thought to your actions, for you have now reached the razor's edge of fate.

CREON

What has happened? I tremble at your voice.

TIRESIAS

You shall know when you have heard the omens
of my art. As I sat on the ancient throne of bird augury,
where my sanctuary gathers every kind of bird,
I heard strange, wild, and frenzied shrieks I could not read,
but I gathered from the sound of whirring wings
that birds were slashing at one another with murderous talons.
I was alarmed, and rushed to place offerings on flaming altars.
But fiery Hephaestus did not blaze forth from the sacrifices;
instead, from the thigh bones we offered, oily drippings oozed
onto the ashes, sputtering and smoking, organs bursting
and spraying their bile into the air, the streaming thigh bones
stripped of the fat in which we had wrapped them.
I was told by this boy that my augury yielded nothing,
for he is my guide, as I am the guide of others.
It is your dogged resolve that has brought suffering to this city.
Birds and dogs have heaped our altars and sacrificial pits
with the flesh of the ill-fated, slaughtered son of Oedipus.
That is why the gods accept neither the prayers that attend

our sacrifices nor the flames from the meat of our offerings.
That is why the birds call out in shrieks I cannot read,
for they have tasted the glistening blood of man.
Give thought to this, my son! All men will err.
But when a man does err, he is not foolish or miserable
if he does not become set in his persistence
but seeks to right the wrong. It is obstinacy
that earns the charge of foolishness. Yield to the dead man,
do not prod and stab a man who has already perished.
What valor is there in killing the dead again?
I say this to you with good will. It is good to learn
from one who is well-disposed, if he is speaking to your profit.

CREON

Venerable elder, you and the others shoot at me like archers
at a target. Your prophetic craft has not left me unscathed.
I have been bartered and sold many times by your kind.
Pursue your profit, sell, if you wish, white gold from Sardis
and gold from India, but you will not bury the dead man in a tomb!
Not even were the eagles of Zeus to seize his carcass for meat
and carry him up to the Olympian throne would I allow
the dead man to be buried in fear of a sacrilegious taint,
for I know that no mortal has the power to taint a god.
Even the cleverest men, aged Tiresias, will fall into disgrace
if they utter in skillful speeches shameful words for their own gain.

TIRESIAS

Alas,
does any man know, does any man consider . . .

CREON

Consider what? What commonplaces will you tell me now?

TIRESIAS

. . . consider how much good counsel is man's greatest wealth?

CREON

To the extent, I am sure, that foolishness is man's greatest affliction.

TIRESIAS

And you are most certainly afflicted with that illness.

CREON

I prefer not to reply with what might disparage a prophet.

TIRESIAS

But you are disparaging me when you say my prophecies are false. 1004

CREON

Prophets are a brood of money-grabbers.

TIRESIAS

Tyrants also tend to corruption.

CREON

Do you realize you are rebuking a king?

TIRESIAS

I do, since it is through my ministrations that you, having saved the city, are king. 1008

CREON

You are an accomplished prophet, but one who favors wrongdoing.

TIRESIAS

You will provoke me to reveal things that lie dormant in my heart.

CREON

Reveal them! As long as you are not revealing them for your own gain.

TIRESIAS

I know you believe I speak for my advantage.

CREON

I assure you that you will never succeed in profiting from how I shall judge.

TIRESIAS

Then know well that within a few courses of the sun's chariot
through the sky you will have to offer as a corpse
one sprung from your own loins, a death in exchange
for a death. You have sent one from here above
to the world below, impiously imprisoning
a living mortal within a grave, while keeping
in this world, without due rituals, without burial rites,
defiled, a corpse that belongs to the infernal gods.
You have no authority over the dead, nor do the gods above,
but by your actions you have done them violence.
For these actions the flesh-ripping Furies
those Avenging Spirits of Hades and the gods above,
are biding their time, lying in ambush for you.
They shall reward you with the same evils
you have brought about. And you think
I tell you this because some man showered me with silver?
A short time will pass, and you shall see your house
filled with the lamentations of man and woman.
All the cities of the Argive league are rising
against you in anger for leaving their dead soldiers
unburied, the mangled corpses with their sacrilegious stench
dragged by dogs and birds back to those cities' hearths.
Since you have provoked me, I have like an archer
shot these arrows in anger at your heart in a steady stream,
and you cannot escape their searing sting.
Boy, lead me home, so that he may unleash
his anger on younger men, and learn
to keep a quieter tongue and a mind ruled

by a sounder judgment than he now displays.

[Exit TIRESIAS, led by the youth]

CHORUS

My Lord, the man has gone after uttering
those terrible prophecies. Since before
my hair turned white from black,
he was never known to proclaim a falsehood to the city.

CREON

I know that, and my mind is in turmoil.
To yield would be terrible, but if I resist
I might allow my passion to be struck down by ruin.

CHORUS

You need to take good counsel, son of Menoeceus.

CREON

What should I do? Tell me, and I shall obey.

CHORUS

Release the maiden from her prison beneath the earth,
and build a tomb for he who lies unburied.

CREON

Is that what you advise? It is best for me to yield?

CHORUS

As quickly as you can, my Lord, for the swift-footed
avengers of the gods cut down those whose judgment errs.

CREON

Alas! It is hard, but I abandon my purpose and will do as you say.
One must not battle in vain against necessity.

CHORUS

You must go and do these things yourself. Do not leave it to others.

CREON

I shall go right away. Come, come, my servants,
every one of you, grab axes and hurry to the place
you see over there. I imprisoned her,
and since I am reversing my decision,
I shall go free her myself. For I have come to believe
that it is best for man to go through life
preserving the established laws.

[Exit CREON]

CHORUS

O god of many names,
pride of the Cadmian bride,*
son of loud-thundering Zeus,
you who haunt the celebrated lands of Italy
and wield power in the valleys
of Eleusinian Demeter that welcome all,
O Bacchus, you who dwell in Thebes,
mother-city of the Bacchants,
by the flowing stream of Ismenus,
by the sowing fields of the savage dragon.[8]

Flashing light and smoky flames
have seen you by the rocky twin peaks
where the Corycian Nymphs, your Bacchants, dance!
The stream of Castalia† has glimpsed you too,
as have the ivy-covered slopes of the Nysaen hills
and the riverbanks green with clustering grapevines.
Divine chants of Euhoe resound
on your procession through the streets of Thebes.

You who honor this city above all others,

---

*Dionysos, son of Zeus and Semele, who was the daughter of Cadmus.

†Stream in Delphi; its water is used for sacred purposes.

you and your mother who was consumed by lightning:
our city and its people
are in the grip of a violent plague!
Come to us once more with cleansing tread,
come over the slopes of Mount Parnassus
or over the wailing waters of the straits.

O great chorus leader
of the fire-breathing stars,
great overseer of the chants
resounding through the night,
son born of Zeus,
appear, O Lord,
with your attendant Thyads,*
who dance in night-long frenzy
for you, Iacchus† the Divine Master!

[Enter MESSENGER]

MESSENGER

Citizens of Thebes, who live by the Houses of Cadmus
and Amphion,‡ nothing lasts within the life of man
that I would ever praise or blame! Fate raises
and Fate topples the lucky and the unlucky,
and there is no prophet for the order that exists.
In my eyes Creon was once to be envied: he saved our land
of Cadmus from our enemies, gained supreme power,
and reigned, thriving through his noble crop of children.
But now all is lost. When a man has been stripped of every joy
I do not regard him as one alive, but see him as a living corpse.
Gather great riches in your house, if you like, and live

---

*Another name for the bacchants, women who celebrate Dionysos with frantic sound and dance.

†Another name for Dionysos.

‡Amphion built the walls of Thebes with his brother Zethos.

with the splendor of a tyrant! But if joy is gone
I would not pay smoke's shadow for all the rest.

CHORUS

What misery for our royal house do you bring us now?

MESSENGER

They are dead, and the living bear the blame for their dying.

CHORUS

Who is the murderer? Who lies dead? Speak!

MESSENGER

Haemon lies slain, his blood spilled by his own—

CHORUS

By his own hand or by the hand of his father?

MESSENGER

By his own hand, enraged by his father's murderous deed.

CHORUS

O prophet, your words have proven true!

MESSENGER

As this has happened, you must convene to decide what must be done.

[EURYDICE comes out of the palace]

CHORUS

I see unhappy Eurydice, Creon's wife!
Is she coming out of the palace just by chance,
or because she has heard about her son?

EURYDICE

My townsmen, as I neared my door to go
in supplication to Pallas Athena with my prayers,
I heard your words. I had just unbolted the door
when the sound of disaster for my house struck my ears.

In fear I fell back and fainted in my servants' arms.
What is the news, repeat it.
I will listen as one not unversed in adversity.

MESSENGER

Beloved queen, I shall tell you, as I myself was there,
and will not leave out a single word of truth.
Why would I comfort you, only later
to be revealed a liar? Truth is always best.
I was escorting your husband to the upper part
of the plain where Polynices' body still lay,
unpitied, torn apart by dogs. We prayed
to Hecate* and Pluto,† to assuage their anger,
and washed and purified the body, gathering up
and burning what remained of it on a pyre
of freshly gathered branches. Over him
we raised a lofty mound of his native soil,
and then proceeded to that bridal chamber
of Hades, with its rock-strewn nuptial bed.
Suddenly one of our men heard in the distance
high-pitched lamentations coming from the maiden's
unsanctified nuptial chamber, and he reported it
to King Creon, who approached, and was engulfed
by confused cries of misery. And he called out in lament,
"O miserable wretch, am I a prophet?
Am I treading the most unfortunate road I have ever traveled?
It is my son's voice that greets me!
Servants, hurry to the tomb! Look through the broken seal
in the mound and tell me if it is Haemon's voice I hear,
or whether the gods are deceiving me!"
At our despairing master's command we looked
into the tomb, and deep within saw her hanging

---

*Goddess of pathways and crossroads.

†Another name for Hades.

by the neck, suspended by a noose of finely woven silk.
By her side, his arms about her waist, Haemon
was lamenting his nuptial bed lost to Hades,
his father's deeds, his marriage destroyed.
Creon sees this, cries out in dreadful lament,
and rushes inside, wailing loudly: "O wretch,
what have you done, what were you thinking?
How is it that you died? Come out, my son,
I beg you as a suppliant!"
But the young man fixes him with savage eyes,
spits in his face, and without reply draws
his double-edged sword, but misses his father,
who runs in flight. The ill-fated boy,
angered at himself, immediately
raises his sword and drives it half its length
into his side. Still alive he clings
to the maiden in faint embrace,
and with his last breath a sudden gush
of blood sprays her white cheek.[9]
There they lie, corpse embracing corpse.
At least he will have his marriage rites in Hades,
poor boy. This proves to mankind how
failing to reason wisely is the greatest evil.

[Exit EURYDICE]

CHORUS

Our queen has left without a single word.
What are we to make of this?

MESSENGER

I too am surprised, but feed on the hope that hearing
of her son's suffering, she does not deem it proper to mourn
before the city, but has retired to her chambers,
where she will have her maidservants bewail the family's grief.
She is not unversed in good judgment,

so she will not do anything that is untoward.

CHORUS

I do not know. Too much silence seems
as dire to me as loud and vain laments.

MESSENGER

I will now go inside the palace, and we shall know
soon enough whether she is keeping something hidden
within a raging heart. But you are right,
there is something dire in so much silence.

[Exit MESSENGER. Enter CREON, carrying the body of his son, followed by attendants.]

CHORUS

Here comes our king himself,
carrying in his arms a striking monument
not of another's recklessness, but of an error
that is all his own, if to say this be allowed.

CREON

Woe,
Stubborn, deadly errors
of unreasonable reason!
You see before you
the killer and the killed,
both of the same blood!
Alas! My disastrous judgment!
Woe, my son, young in your untimely death,
Ai ai! Ai ai!
You are dead, you are gone,
not because of your bad judgment
but because of mine.

CHORUS

Alas! You seem to have seen justice too late.

CREON

Alas!
Poor wretch, I have learned my lesson.
A god had struck me on the head with all his might,
casting me into ways of cruelty—alas!—
and has torn down my joy, crushing it underfoot!
Ah! Ah! The agony and pain of mortals!

[Enter MESSENGER from the palace]

MESSENGER

O my Lord! You come bearing great sorrow with you,
but will harvest even more: one you are carrying in your arms,
while another awaits you in the palace when you enter.

CREON

What worse can follow an evil such as this?

MESSENGER

Your wife is dead, a mother to the last to your perished son.
The unhappy woman died by blows she herself just now
inflicted.

CREON

Woe!
Woe! Harbor of Hades impossible to cleanse,
why, why are you destroying me?

[To the MESSENGER]

You who bring me these evil tidings,
what are you telling me?
Ai ai! You are killing a man already dead.
What are you saying, boy?
What new death are you reporting?
Ai ai! Ai ai!
my wife's death, as slaughter
upon slaughter entangles me?

CHORUS

You can see her. She is no longer hidden within the palace.

CREON

Alas!
I see the second evil, poor wretch that I am.
What fate, oh what fate still awaits me?
I am bearing my son in my arms, poor wretch that I am,
and now I see her lying before me, dead.
Woe, woe, pitiful mother! Woe, my son!

MESSENGER

Here before the altar, with sharpened knife,
she released her eyes into darkness, after lamenting
the empty bed of Megareus who had died before,
and that of Haemon, finally calling down every evil
upon you as the killer of your son.

CREON

Ai ai! Ai ai!
I quake with dread! Why does not someone strike me
in the heart with a double-edged sword?
I am miserable—
ai ai!—dissolving in misery.

MESSENGER

The woman lying here dead charged you
with the deaths of this son and the other too.

CREON

How did she shed her blood?

MESSENGER

By driving with her own hand a knife into her breast
when she heard of the boy's bitter misfortune.

CREON

Woe! Woe! The guilt will ever be mine

and none other's. I killed you, O misery,
it was I, it is true!
Take me away, my servants, as quickly as you can,
take me far away, I am nothing.

CHORUS

What you say is good, if there can be good within such evil,
for the evils at hand are best dealt with quickly.

CREON

Let it come. Let it come.
Let violent death be the supreme fate
bringing me my final day.
Let it come. Let it come!
May I never see another day.

CHORUS

These things are of the future. What lies before us now
must be our concern. Leave the rest to others.

CREON

What I prayed for is what I wish.

CHORUS

Do not pray at all. Mortals
cannot escape their destiny.

CREON

Lead me away! I am the rash man who killed you,
my son, and you too, my wife. Alas, wretch that I am,
I cannot look on either of you, I have nothing to hold onto.
Everything these hands have touched has turned to grief
and fate has come down upon my head.

[Exit CREON and attendants]

CHORUS

Good judgment is by far the first principle
of happiness. One must not act impiously

in what concerns the gods.
Great words bring great blows to men
who are proud, teaching them 1284
good judgment in their old age.

ENDNOTES

OEDIPUS THE KING

1. (l. 3) *with the garlanded branches of suppliants:* Supplication was a desperate request for assistance from a god. The implication is that the Theban citizens have come to Oedipus as their last resort. They are led by the priest of Zeus, the supreme Greek god, which points to the high expectations they have for their ruler's intervention.
2. (l. 88) *Speak out to all. I lament for my people:* These lines effectively turn the quest for Laius' killer into a public investigation under the eyes of the citizens. Even though the rest of the play focuses on Oedipus' own progress toward the truth of his origins, it is important to remember that he cannot turn back on his commitment to search for the killer, or conduct the search privately.
3. (l. 125) *The Sphinx singing her deadly riddles:* The Sphinx that terrorized Thebes (see the Introduction) is brought in here again as a plot device, in order to explain why the investigation of Laius' murder had not been conducted earlier.
4. (l. 369) *Whose inventions are these? Creon's?:* It is perhaps only natural for Oedipus to suspect Creon, for the truth that Tiresias reveals is completely unexpected and difficult to accept, while Creon's designs to become the ruler of Thebes are to be expected, given his relation to the royal family.
5. (l. 624) *You cannot turn this trifling matter into something great:* The matter is, of course, hardly trifling. Is Jocasta trying to stop one more quarrel of the many that she has witnessed between Oedipus and Creon, or is she trying to turn the whole discussion into

a private affair that she can influence more easily inside the doors of the royal palace?

6. (ll. 803–804) *But until you hear from the man who was present, have hope:* It is as though the chorus spoke to Oedipus and to themselves, for the truth is much too hard to accept, and it is tempting to seek further evidence from material witnesses.
7. (l. 1022) *Unfortunate man, may you never find out who you are:* At this point Jocasta must at least have strong suspicions about the truth, but she seems to prefer to ignore it, and in contrast with Oedipus, she would presumable be able to do so.
8. (ll. 1231–1232) *He tore off the golden pins that fastened her dress, raised them high, . . .:* By so doing, Jocasta's naked breasts would have been exposed. Only now, with the knowledge of her identity, Oedipus cannot bear that sight. His self-blinding actions, therefore, are directly related to this moment (which would not have appeared on stage, but is told to us by a messenger, as usual in Greek tragedy).

OEDIPUS AT COLONUS

1. (l. 55) *The ground on which you stand is called the Bronze Threshold:* Oedipus is standing on the entrance to the underworld, which, according to Homer, is made of bronze. Hence the concurrent references to the Titans, older gods thrown into the underworld by Zeus and the new Olympian gods, and to Prometheus, who stole fire from Zeus in order to give it to men.
2. (ll. 92–93) *I . . . would never in all my journeys have encountered you first, abstemious goddesses:* The Eumenides are called "abstemious" because libations poured in their honor were not made with wine, contrary to what was customary in sacred rites for other gods.
3. (l. 212) *what he has first been made to suffer:* The chorus means that Oedipus has tricked them by not disclosing immediately that he is cursed and polluted. Therefore, they are not bound by their earlier promise to him.
4. (l. 517) *I am guiltless. I did not know who he was:* This is, of course, the obvious defense, even though Oedipus does not use it at all in

Oedipus the King. His change of attitude should perhaps be understood in connection with the outlook on life given in the speech on old age in lines 1182–1221.

5. (l. 923) *I knew that the Council of the Areopagus of this land:* This is an allusion to the highest criminal court in archaic Athens. It plays a prominent role in the final acquittal of Orestes in Aeschylus' *Eumenides*.
6. (l. 1039) *the beloved son of Rhea:* The reference is to Okeanos, one of the earliest gods to appear in Hesiod's *Theogony* and whose birth is linked to the creation of the world. The ancient Greeks believed that the whole earth was encircled by him.
7. (l. 1286) *who remained a virgin until she finally conceived her trusted son:* "Parthenopaius" means "son of an unmarried girl." More generally, the listing of all the allies that Polynices has gathered justifies his decision to march on to Thebes later, even without his father's support.
8. (ll. 1493–1494) *will never be destroyed by the Sown Men:* According to the myth of the founding of Thebes, Cadmus had sown the teeth of a dragon, from which warriors sprung who helped Cadmus establish the city; it later was walled by Amphion and Zethos.
9. (l. 1549) *where the covenant of Theseus and Perithous is honored:* We don't know all of what is meant by these details (although Sophocles' audience must have, of course). We do know that Theseus and Perithous attempted to rescue Persephone from Hades, but they failed and were imprisoned there, though later they were rescued by Herakles. The "covenant" mentioned here obviously relates to the fine points of the division between the realms of the living and the dead.

ANTIGONE

1. (l. 140) *in homage to Zeus, bringer of victory:* In archaic Greek warfare, a trophy (*tropaion*) was set up on the spot where the enemy had been routed. The trophy consisted of the enemy's combat gear, conspicuously displayed on wooden stands.
2. (l. 320) *but none more wondrous than man:* This choral song is known

as the "Hymn to Man." Notice how it contains both expressions of wonder about human achievements and a reminder of the limits of human action, which Creon transgresses in the play.

3. (l. 652) *. . . then better by a man. May we not be called inferior to a woman:* If Creon acts only, or mostly, out of fear of being bested by a woman, this may well be his tragic mistake (*hamartia*, on which see the Introduction); that would support the view that Creon is the hero of the play, instead of Antigone.
4. (l. 789) *I have heard that the daughter of Tantalus . . . :* Antigone refers to Niobe, wife of the Theban Amphion. Niobe was punished by Leto (Apollo's mother) after Niobe boasted about bearing many more children than the goddess. Leto killed Niobe's children, and Niobe returned to her father in Phrygia. Out of pity for her, the gods turned her into stone. Perhaps Antigone speaks of Niobe as another suffering woman who passes from life to death without violence.
5. (l. 905) *Danae too suffered Fate's yoke:* The three examples in this choral song are of characters of high birth who were nevertheless made to suffer by fate. Danae was imprisoned by her father, the king of Argos, when he learned from an oracle that he would be killed by his daughter's son. Zeus, however, found a way to impregnate her by changing himself into a golden rain. She later gave birth to Perseus, who would eventually fulfill the prophecy.
6. (l. 916) *Fate also tamed the hotheaded son of Dryas, . . . :* This is a reference to Lykourgos, imprisoned by Dionysos for the killing of his own son. There are several versions of this story, and it is hard to know which one is meant here.
7. (l. 932) *by the king's wild wife:* This is a reference to a story we do not know very well. It is probably the tale of Kleopatra, daughter of Boreas, who marries Phineus and bears him two sons; afterward he divorces her and takes a new wife who blinds her stepchildren.
8. (l. 1076) *by the sowing fields of the savage dragon:* See note 8 to *Oedipus at Colonus*.
9. (ll. 1176–1177) *a sudden gush of blood sprays her white cheek:* This scene involves a reverse sex simile that requires some explanation.

Antigone has confronted Creon and taken on a powerful attitude more proper to a male, while Haemon has been more pliant and has lost his bride as a result. Antigone has hung herself (a typical woman's death in Greek tragedy), and Haemon dies by his own sword (a typical man's death), but in the final moment it is the man's blood that stains the woman, in a reversal of what would have happened if the marriage had actually taken place and been consummated.

Inspired by
THREE THEBAN PLAYS

As some of the best-known and most compelling stories in world literature, the plays of Sophocles have been widely adapted. Directors have taken approaches that range from painstaking recreations of ancient Greek theater to wildly modern, free-form versions.

British director Tyrone Guthrie provides an excellent opportunity for modern viewers to experience historically accurate Greek drama in his filmed version of *Oedipus Rex* (1957). Mirroring what the conditions of ancient Greek theater were understood to be in the 1950s, Guthrie adorns his players with eerie, grotesque masks and moves them about the stage in a solemn, stylized choreography. The experienced cast, members of the Shakespearean Festival Players of Stratford, Ontario, features Douglas Campbell as Oedipus, Eleanor Stuart as Jocasta, and a young William Shatner as a (masked) member of the chorus. Following a script translated by William Butler Yeats, the characters speak in a rhythmic, ceremonial manner, emphasizing their lack of autonomy in the face of divine prophecy.

In a decided departure from historical authenticity, controversial Italian director Pier Paolo Pasolini chose the Moroccan desert as the backdrop for his visceral, surreal *Edipo Re* (*Oedipus Rex*; 1967). Franco Citti plays an unrestrained, psychotic Oedipus, driven by primeval emotions. The characters, including Silvana Mangano as Jocasta, inhabit a stunningly filmed, prehistoric-looking landscape, and wear highly ornamented tribal costumes and bizarre headgear. The film is said to be autobiographical—the director despised his father—and feels as if it emerged straight from the gut. Praised for its raw artistic power, *Edipo Re* trades strict interpretation of Sophocles for an intensely personal take on the drama.

For his acclaimed black-and-white *Antigoni* (*Antigone*; 1961), Greek writer-director George Tzavellas employed traditional moviemaking technique. Instead of a handful of masked, rigid performers, he used thousands of soldiers and citizens in period costumes. The sight of Creon's enormous army brings home the incredible power wielded by the ill-fated ruler, as the action of the story unfolds on the screen rather than solely through narrative. Foregoing formality in favor of more naturalistic performances, Iréne Papas is a powerful, moving Antigone, and an equally adept Manos Katrakis plays Creon.

Playwright Jean Anouilh's modern interpretation of *Antigone*, which deemphasizes the role of fate, stemmed from parallels the writer saw between the rule of Creon and the Nazi-installed Vichy government in France during World War II. Produced in 1974 as part of the PBS Great Performances series, director Gerald Freedman's filmed version of the play is set among the stark streets and cold governmental offices of an authoritarian state. Fritz Weaver as Creon and Geneviève Bujold as Antigone provide intense performances that highlight the dangers of blind idealism in politics. Another important version of *Antigone* was the one produced by Bertolt Brecht in 1948, in which Creon was portrayed as a much more manipulative character than in Sophocles' play. Brecht's version is available in an English translation by Judith Malina.

Igor Stravinsky wrote a majestic, two-act opera of *Oedipus Rex* (1928) that features a libretto by French writer Jean Cocteau. Tony Award–winning director Julie Taymor's much-admired television version of the opera appeared in 1993 and won an Emmy for costume design. With a script by Gabriel García Márquez, director Jorge Alí Triana's *Edipo Alcalde* (*Mayor Oedipus*; 1996) transports *Oedipus the King* to a violent, strife-torn village in the mountains of Colombia.

The Gospel at Colonus, a musical set in a black Pentecostal church, is one of the only filmed versions of *Oedipus at Colonus*. Morgan Freeman plays the Messenger in this excellent production, which aired on PBS in 1985. Not for the faint of heart, Amy Greenfield's experimental, multimedia modern dance film *Antigone/Rites of Passion* (1990) features exotic imagery and an avant-garde rock soundtrack. Reliable adaptations on the more traditional end of the spectrum include the BBC trilogy that aired in 1984, translated and directed by Don Taylor, and Philip Saville's *Oedipus the King* (1967), which stars Christopher Plummer as Oedipus, Lilli Palmer as Jocasta, and Orson Welles as Tiresias.

Versions and adaptations of Greek tragedy have also appeared in Africa. *Oedipus the King* is the basis for Nigerian author Ola Rotimi's play *The Gods Are Not to Blame* (1968), which incorporates folk wisdom and songs in Yoruba, while *Antigone* is the loud-beating heart of Athol Fugard's *The Island* (1972), an extremely powerful anti-apartheid play from South Africa. The political content of Greek tragedy is one of the main reasons for its continued literary success and permanence on the stage. In addition to the versions mentioned above, interested readers should check their local theater listings, in which productions of Greek tragedy and modern adaptations appear surprisingly often.

COMMENTS & QUESTIONS

In this section, we aim to provide the reader with an array of perspectives on the texts, as well as questions that challenge those perspectives. The commentary has been culled from sources as diverse as comments contemporaneous with the works, literary criticism of later generations, and appreciations written throughout the works' history. Following the commentary, a series of questions seeks to filter Three Theban Plays *through a variety of points of view and bring about a richer understanding of these enduring works.*

COMMENTS

Aristotle

Sophocles said that he drew men as they ought to be; Euripides, as they are.

—from the *Poetics* (fourth century B.C.),
as translated by S. H. Butcher

Karl Wilhelm Friedrich von Schlegel

In every species of intellectual developmen—(as in the visible gradations of the physical world)—there is one short period of complete bloom—one highest point of fulness and perfection—which is manifested, at the moment of its existence, by the beauty and faultlessness of the form and the language in which it is embodied. This point, not in the art of composing tragedies alone, but in the whole poetry and mental refinement of the Greeks, is the period of Sophocles. In him we find an overflowing fullness of that indescribable charm of which we can perceive only rare specimens in the writings of most other poets and writers—but which, whenever we do find it, we at once, by intuition as it were, recognize to be the symbol of perfection, whether it makes its appearance in the structure of thought or the style of language. Through the transparent beauty of his works we can perceive the internal harmony and beauty of his soul.

—from *Lectures on the History of Literature, Ancient and Modern* (1815), as translated by John Lockhart Gibson

Georg Wilhelm Friedrich Hegel

[Tragic reconciliation] is most complete when the individuals . . . violate what, if they were true to their own nature, they should be honouring. For example, Antigone lives under the political authority of Creon; she is herself the daughter of a King and the fiancée of Haemon, so that she ought to pay obedience to the royal command. But Creon too, as father and husband, should have respected the sacred tie of blood and not ordered anything against its pious observance. So there is immanent in both Antigone and Creon something that in their own way they attack, so that they are gripped and shattered by something intrinsic to their own actual being. Of all the masterpieces of the classical and the modern world—and I know nearly all of them and you should and can—the *Antigone* seems to me to be the most magnificent and satisfying work of art of this kind.

—from *Aesthetics* (1835), as translated by T. M. Knox

Johann Peter Eckermann and Johann Wolfgang von Goethe

Wed., Mar. 28. [1827]—We then conversed further upon Sophocles, remarking that in his pieces he always less considered a moral tendency than an apt treatment of the subject in hand, particularly with regard to theatrical effect.

"I do not object," said Goethe, "to a dramatic poet having a moral influence in view; but when the point is to bring his subject clearly and effectively before his audience, his moral purpose proves of little use, and he needs much more a faculty for delineation and a familiarity with the stage to know what to do and what to leave undone. If there be a moral in the subject, it will appear, and the poet has nothing to consider but the effective and artistic treatment of his subject. If a poet has as high a soul as Sophocles, his influence will always be moral, let him do what he will. Besides, he knew the stage, and understood his craft thoroughly."

—from *Conversations with Eckermann* (1836),
as translated by John Oxenford

Matthew Arnold

In Sophocles what is valuable is not so much his contributions to psychology and the anatomy of sentiment, as the grand moral effects produced by *style*. For the style is the expression of the nobility of the poet's character, as the matter is the expression of the richness of his mind: but on men character produces as great an effect as mind.

—from a letter to Arthur Hugh Clough (March 1849)

Friedrich Nietzsche

Sophocles understood the most sorrowful figure of the Greek stage, the unfortunate Oedipus, as the noble human being who, in spite of his wisdom, is destined to error and misery but who eventually, through his tremendous suffering, spreads a magical power of blessing that remains effective even beyond his decease. The noble human being does not sin, the profound poet wants to tell us: though every law, every natural order, even the moral world may perish through his actions, his actions also produce a higher magical circle of effects which found a new world on the ruins of the old one that has been overthrown. . . . As a poet he first shows us a marvelously tied knot of a trial, slowly unraveled by the judge, bit by bit, for his own undoing. The genuinely Hellenic delight at this dialectical solution is so great that it introduces a trait of superior cheerfulness into the whole work, everywhere softening the sharp points of the gruesome presuppositions of this process.

—from *The Birth of Tragedy* (1872),
as translated by Walter Kaufmann

John Addington Symonds

The drama of Sophocles sets forth a complete view of human destiny as conceived by the most perfect of Greek intellects.

—from *Studies of the Greek Poets* (1873)

Sir Richard Claverhouse Webb

Sophocles has been described, in well-known words, as one "who saw life steadily, and saw it whole." Those words, true of his dramatic art, are equally true of his religious and moral ideas. He saw the evil and sorrow that are in life as part of a divine scheme, which may, indeed, appoint such discipline for the good of the individual, but which also subordinates the welfare of the individual to the welfare of the race.

—from *The Growth and Influence of Classical Greek Poetry* (1893)

Thomas Hardy

If the mean age for the best *literary* work is thirty-seven it must be owing to the conditions of modern life; for we are told that Homer sang when old and blind, while Æschylus wrote his best tragedies when over sixty, Sophocles some of his best when nearly ninety, and Euripides did not begin to write till forty, and went on to seventy; and in these you have the pick of the greatest poets who ever lived.

—from a letter to Hall Caine (January 29, 1918)

Sigmund Freud

The *Oedipus Tyrannus* is a so-called tragedy of fate; its tragic effect is said to be found in the opposition between the powerful will of the gods and the vain resistance of the human beings who are threatened with destruction; resignation to the will of God and confession of one's helplessness is the lesson which the deeply-moved spectator is to learn from the tragedy. Consequently modern authors have tried to obtain a similar tragic effect by embodying the same opposition in a story of their own invention. But spectators have sat unmoved while a curse or an oracular sentence has been fulfilled on blameless human beings in spite of all their struggles; later tragedies of fate have all remained without effect.

If the *Oedipus Tyrannus* is capable of moving modern men no less than it moved the contemporary Greeks, the explanation of this fact cannot lie merely in the assumption that the effect of the Greek tragedy is based upon the opposition between fate and human will, but is to be sought in the peculiar nature of the material by which the opposition is shown.

There must be a voice within us which is prepared to recognize the compelling power of fate in *Oedipus*, while we justly condemn the situations occurring in *Die Ahnfrau* or in other tragedies of later date as arbitrary inventions. And there must be a factor corresponding to this inner voice in the story of King Oedipus. His fate moves us only for the reason that it might have been ours, for the oracle has put the same curse upon us before our birth as upon him. Perhaps we are all destined to direct our first sexual impulses towards our mothers, and our first hatred and violent wishes towards our fathers; our dreams convince us of it. King Oedipus, who has struck his father Laius dead and has married his mother Jocasta, is nothing but the realised wish of our childhood. But more fortunate than he, we have since succeeded, unless we have become psychoneurotics, in withdrawing our sexual impulses from our mothers and in forgetting our jealousy of our fathers. We recoil from the person for whom this primitive wish has been fulfilled with all the force of the repression which these wishes have suffered within us. By his analysis, showing us the guilt of Oedipus, the poet urges us to recognise our own inner self, in which these impulses, even if suppressed, are still present.

—from *The Interpretation of Dreams* (1899),
as translated by A. A. Brill

Virginia Woolf

In six pages of Proust we can find more complicated and varied emotions than in the whole of the *Electra*. But in the *Electra* or in the *Antigone* we are impressed by something different, by something perhaps more impressive—by heroism itself, by fidelity itself. In spite of the labour and the difficulty it is this that draws us back and back to the Greeks; the stable, the permanent, the original human being is to be found there.

—from *The Common Reader* (1925)

QUESTIONS

Oedipus the King

1. Could Oedipus have ignored the Theban citizens' request for assistance? What would the consequences have been?

2. Jocasta seems distraught by Oedipus' search for Laius' killer. Did she suspect the truth from the beginning? Could she have continued living with it after Oedipus found it out?

3. Tiresias certainly seems to have known Oedipus' identity well in advance. Why didn't he warn Oedipus?

Oedipus at Colonus

4. How is the old Oedipus different from the younger man? Is it only knowledge about his origins that has made him different?

5. Compare the characters of Antigone and Ismene. Which one is closer to Oedipus? Is there any way to anticipate which one will have a greater role to play in *Antigone*?

6. Compare Creon and Theseus. Can you tell whether one is more self-serving than the other in their attempts to give Oedipus shelter?

7. The circumstances of Oedipus' death are not very clear. What problems are avoided by not revealing the place of his death? What advantages may be gained by keeping it secret?

Antigone

8. Would Creon's decision not to bury Polynices be considered a cruel act today? Why or why not?

9. Is Antigone's position a rational one? Was there a way in which she could have compromised with Creon and saved her life? If so, why doesn't she pursue it?

10. Consider Haemon's attitude about Antigone's punishment. Is it understandable? How does the play portray the balance of his obligation toward his father, Creon, and his anticipated new life as Antigone's husband?

FOR FURTHER READING

WORKS MENTIONED IN THE INTRODUCTION

Aristotle. *Poetics.* Translated by P. H. Epps. Chapel Hill: University of North Carolina Press, 1942.

Burian, P. "Myth into *Muthos*: The Shaping of Tragic Plots." In *The Cambridge Companion to Greek Tragedy*, edited by P. E. Easterling. Cambridge: Cambridge University Press, 1997, pp. 178–208.

Freud, S. *The Interpretation of Dreams.* Edited by R. Robertson; translated by J. Crick. Oxford and New York: Oxford University Press, 1999.

Knox, B. "Introduction." In *Sophocles: The Three Theban Plays.* Translated by R. Fagles. New York: Penguin Classics, 2000.

GENERAL WORKS ON GREEK TRAGEDY

Easterling, P. E. *The Cambridge Companion to Greek Tragedy.* Cambridge: Cambridge University Press, 1997. A very good collection of papers by different scholars on many aspects of tragedy, with an extensive bibliography.

Foley, H. P. *Female Acts in Greek Tragedy.* Princeton, NJ: Princeton University Press, 2001.

Goldhill, S. *Reading Greek Tragedy.* Cambridge and New York: Cambridge University Press, 1986.

Hall, E. *Inventing the Barbarian: Greek Self-Definition through Tragedy.* Oxford and New York: Oxford University Press, 1989.

Knox, B. *Word and Action: Essays on the Ancient Theater.* Baltimore, MD: Johns Hopkins University Press, 1979.

Sourvinou-Inwood, C. *Tragedy and Athenian Religion.* Lanham, MD: Lexington Books, 2003.

Taplin, O. *Greek Tragedy in Action.* Second edition. London and New York: Routledge, 2003.

Vernant, J.-P., and P. Vidal-Naquet. *Myth and Tragedy in Ancient Greece.* Translated by J. Lloyd. New York: Zone Books, 1990. One of the best studies of the relationship between myth and tragedy.

Wiles, D. *Greek Theatre Performance: An Introduction.* Cambridge and New York: Cambridge University Press, 2000.

Winkler, J. J., and F. I. Zeitlin, eds. *Nothing to Do with Dionysos? Athenian Drama in Its Social Context.* Princeton, NJ: Princeton University Press, 1990.

PHILOSOPHICAL INTERPRETATIONS OF TRAGEDY

Aristotle. *Poetics.* Translation and commentary by S. Halliwell. Chapel Hill: University of North Carolina Press, 1987.

Eagleton, T. *Sweet Violence: The Idea of the Tragic.* Malden, MA: Blackwell, 2003.

Kaufman, W. *Tragedy and Philosophy.* Garden City, NY: Doubleday, 1968.

Murray, P., ed. *Plato on Poetry.* Cambridge Greek and Latin Classics. Cambridge and New York: Cambridge University Press, 1996. This book requires knowledge of Greek beyond the introduction, which is worth reading on its own.

Nuttall, A. D. *Why Does Tragedy Give Pleasure?* Oxford and New York: Oxford University Press, 1996.

MODERN PRODUCTIONS OF GREEK TRAGEDY

Hartigan, K. V. *Greek Tragedy on the American Stage: Ancient Drama in the Commercial Theater, 1882–1994.* Westport, CT: Greenwood Press, 1995.

MacKinnon, K. *Greek Tragedy into Film.* London: Croom Helm, 1986.

SOPHOCLES

Knox, B. *The Heroic Temper: Studies in Sophoclean Tragedy.* Sather Classical Lectures, Vol. 35. Berkeley: University of California Press, 1964.

Reinhardt, K. *Sophocles.* Oxford: Blackwell, 1979.

Winnington-Ingram, R. P. *Sophocles: An Interpretation.* Cambridge and New York: Cambridge University Press, 1980.

WORKS ON THE PLAYS IN THIS VOLUME

Burian, P. "Suppliant and Savior: Oedipus at Colonus." *Phoenix* 28 (1974), pp. 408–429.

Butler, J. *Antigone's Claim: Kinship between Life and Death.* New York: Columbia University Press, 2002. A reading of the play that explores its validity as a model for feminist and/or radical politics.

Knox, B. *Oedipus at Thebes: Sophocles' Tragic Hero and His Time.* New Haven, CT: Yale University Press, 1998.

Steiner, G. *Antigones.* Oxford: Oxford University Press, 1984. Superb coverage of the play's successive interpretations and adaptations.

In addition, readers who can read classical Greek may wish to consult the following editions of the texts with critical commentary.

Dawe, R. D., ed. *Sophocles: Oedipus Rex.* Second edition. Cambridge Greek and Latin Classics. Cambridge and New York: Cambridge University Press, 2006.

Griffith, M., ed. *Sophocles: Antigone.* Cambridge Greek and Latin Classics. Cambridge and New York: Cambridge University Press, 1999.

OTHER TRANSLATIONS OF THE PLAYS IN THIS VOLUME

Fagles, R., trans. *Sophocles: The Three Theban Plays.* With an introduction and notes by Bernard Knox. New York: Penguin Classics, 2000.

Fitts, D., and R. Fitzgerald, trans. *Sophocles. The Oedipus Cycle: Oedipus Rex, Oedipus at Colonus, Antigone.* New York: Harvest Books, 1949.

Grene, D., and R. Lattimore. *The Complete Greek Tragedies: Sophocles.* Vol. 1. Chicago: University of Chicago Press, 1991.